On Our Way Home

On Our Way Home

MIKE FLORIO

ALSO BY MIKE FLORIO

Playmakers
(PublicAffairs, 2022)

Father of Mine
(2023)

30 America Avenue
(TBD)

Big Shield
(TBD)

Used Carrs
(TBD)

Son of Mine
(TBD)

Paperback ISBN: 979-8-9879440-3-5

Ebook ISBN: 979-8-9879440-2-8

To Anthony and Maggie

1

STAYING UP LATE sucks.

When I was a little kid, staying up late was a bonus, a luxury. A treat. There was an unpredictability to it. That made it even more exciting when it actually happened.

Most of the time, Baby Michael and I would get a "no." Not even a "no," just that look from Mom or Dad. Usually Dad. The one that made it crystal clear we shouldn't even bother to finish asking the question.

Bedtime was an obligation that applied even when there wasn't anything to get up for, because our house was too small for parents to properly sleep (or periodically not go to sleep right away) if their two young boys wrestled and argued and argued and wrestled deep into the night. Not that we ever made a lot of noise when we got to stay up late. Neither of us were all that smart, but we were bright enough to know that breaking glass or smashing furniture after midnight would result in fewer chances to ever do it again.

I don't remember much about the things Baby Michael and I actually did when we stayed up late, because I'd quit thinking about those nights. I'd quit thinking about those nights, because I'd quit thinking about Baby Michael. I'd quit thinking about Baby Michael, because I'd become extremely and permanently pissed off at Grown-up Michael.

For Grown-up John, staying up late is the exact opposite of bonus, luxury, or treat. I need my sleep. And there's nothing fun about being awake after eleven o'clock. Not anymore.

Staying up that late now means I've got a trial starting soon, or I'm in the middle of one. It also means no sleeping in on the other side of staying up. I never did sleep deprivation well. I've gradually learned to live with it. It's a debt that eventually gets paid off, at some point when life gets back to normal.

I'm not sure that I've ever fully reconciled those deficits. Maybe I'll finally balance out the ledger when I'm in the old folks' home, when there will be nothing else to do other than smear pudding on my bib or dump crap in my pants. Or both. Maybe at the same time. Maybe that's when I'll pay off that sleep debt. Just in time to go to sleep for good.

The accounts payable had spiked again lately, thanks to the double whammy of a trial coming to an end on Friday and Christmas Eve landing two days later. With three kids—fifteen, twelve, five—things that as of the morning of December 22 I didn't even know had been bought by my wife would have to be *some-assembly-required* in that sliver of time between the lights going out upstairs and the youngest one springing awake to a non-stop, jabbering frenzy of activity. To make things worse, Macy (whose *full-and-complete-assembly-required* bike was hidden in a cardboard box under the workbench in the garage) had already begun hounding Linda about going to midnight mass, a legitimate occasion to stay up late even though the girl would transform into a sweaty clump of eye boogers well before I heard the term from Isaiah 9:6 that never made any sense to me.

Wonder-Counselor.

Whatever it meant, it sounded exactly like what I needed to be that morning. The trial had started on Monday. The lawyers representing the company had asked for a delay on the Tuesday before Thanksgiving. I'd given the maximum contribution to the judge's two campaigns just for times like this. They're not supposed to know who gives what and how much, but the full list of donations becomes public record, and it's way too easy to give in to the temptation to check. So I gave to the limit, Linda gave to the limit, her parents gave to the limit, and mine would have given to the limit, too, if both hadn't been gone for more than two decades.

We all gave to the limit so that, for example, a random collection of local residents would get to decide two days before Christmas Eve whether one of their own had her rights violated by a rich, powerful, and faceless corporation. Sure, the company provides jobs for hundreds in the area. It also fires people from those jobs without regard to the requirements of the law. And it sucks tens of millions of dollars in raw profit out of the state, every single month.

The idea of handing a wrongful termination case to a jury on the 22nd of December sounded very good, in theory. I'd always wanted to do it, but I could never get the dominoes to fall the right way.

When the judge had held the scheduling conference sixteen months earlier, I could sense the assorted dates and deadlines for the litigation pointing toward the end of the year. I suggested December 18 for the start of the trial. The low-level, billable-hours-churning, fresh-from-law-school underling who'd been given the lead partner's calendar didn't realize that beginning a trial on that day would result in the jury getting the case dangerously close to Christmas, and that I'd then spend the entire week clanging a bell next to a red kettle, a Robin Hood who'd swapped his green hat for a red cap trimmed in white.

I know how that sounds. I do. But that's the way it works. Good lawyers secure every possible edge for their clients. If there was any way I could nudge the process toward the jury returning a big verdict in the matter of *Matherson vs. U-Sav-Plentee, Inc. et al.* so close to Christmas, I wouldn't have been representing my client the right way if I hadn't at least tried to do it.

I'd succeeded. I got the date, and I fought off the motion for a continuance. I probably was a little too much of a jerk when pointing out that if Mr. Anderson had planned to go out of town for the holidays on December 20, he shouldn't have allowed his junior associate to agree to start the trial that week—or maybe he should have participated in the scheduling conference himself. But here's the thing. Proper representation of a client in litigation requires being a little too much of a jerk, pretty much all the time.

So that's how it went. In the months before the trial started, I questioned thirteen U-Sav-Plentee employees in the cramped conference room of my law office. The company's lawyers produced more than fourteen thousand documents for me to review, since they always bury a handful of needles as deep in the haystack as they can.

They eventually filed what's known as a motion for summary judgment. It forced me to put together a twenty-page legal brief that turned over just enough of my cards to show there was more than enough evidence of wrongdoing to support a jury verdict for Sandy Matherson. Along the way, we attended a court-ordered mediation session that made no progress at all toward a settlement, mainly because the manager of the local store barely had the power to go to the bathroom without first calling corporate headquarters for permission. After all of that, the case went to trial as scheduled.

Being at trial can be exhilarating. Getting ready for trial blows. It takes hours and hours and hours of concentrated effort, usually at night and on weekends because the rest of your practice doesn't take a hiatus. Trial prep requires focus, resilience, perseverance. It needs a careful eye, scanning every relevant piece of information, over and over and over again for anything that can be used to support the arguments being made on behalf of a client, and to avoid a sawed-off shotgun of attacks being fired by the other side. It's much more than knowing how to present your own case; it's about understanding how their case will unfold, while also being ready to swing at any and all curve balls that may or may not be heading directly for your temple.

They might dig up dirt on your client from years before she even got the job. They might pull a key document out of nowhere, after hiding it from you for months. One of the jurors could bow out, because a kid suddenly has the flu. In comes the alternate juror, and the whole dynamic of the group changes.

I had to be ready for anything and everything, all the time. I had to have a plan for dealing with any and all wrinkles. If I didn't have a plan, I had to come up with one. If I couldn't come up with one, I had to act like I had one. And I had to do it all while staying up late and getting up early, night after night after night.

Why was I still doing this? I started off working for a big law firm that represented employers. I became a partner. Impressive title. More money. I didn't care. I wanted to handle cases I believed in. Lawyers who work at big firms have to handle the cases that get filed against their clients, no matter how good or bad those cases might be.

For me, more often than not, they were bad. I didn't believe in them. So I'd work on the case until the time was right to explain to the client why the case should be settled. That alone was an art. Telling the client that it needs to write a check to make a case go away too early in the process comes off as weakness. Waiting too long invites questions like, "Why didn't you tell us this sooner?"

For defense firms, the business creates an incentive to keep a case alive as long as possible. Lawyers who represent corporations get paid for their time. If a case goes away too quickly, there's much less time to be spent and, as a result, much less money to be made. The goal, even with a stinker of a case, is to let enough of the litigation play out before telling the client the time has come to broker a deal. Legal fees fully earned, problem fully solved, justice fully done. Or whatever. Regardless, I got no pleasure from handling dying-dog cases that, sooner or later, would be put out of their misery, and mine.

Now that I'd hung a shingle and practiced alone, I got to screen the cases. Pick the cases I felt good about. Accept the cases that seemed to be rooted in truth, fairness, and righteousness.

The cases also had to carry a good chance of kicking out some cold, hard cash. Practicing law is still a for-profit enterprise. Fighting for principle never kept the lights on or the kids fed. The cases I took needed to include rights that were violated, financial losses that were real, and a defendant that could pay without batting an eye. Otherwise, it just wasn't worth the time, the effort, or the money required to get a case ready to present to a jury.

In *Matherson vs. U-Sav-Plentee, Inc. et al.*, the numbers made sense. U-Sav-Plentee was one of the biggest companies in the world. It had billions on the balance sheet. It made millions more every day.

For the company, this case was a one-winged gnat, not even rising to the level of gently mild annoyance. Whatever the verdict might be, it'd fall far short of the interest earned in a single day on the loose cash the company kept in its worldwide bank accounts. But U-Sav-Plentee still fought Sandy Matherson aggressively and zealously, because that's what companies like that do. If they didn't, every employee with any complaint of any kind would line up for their own chance at what the company viewed as a lottery prize, not as fair compensation for the misbehavior of its poorly-trained, randomly-supervised, and/or badly-intentioned local managers.

At trial, I had to show that U-Sav-Plentee fired Sandy Matherson not because she had a habit of clocking in more than fifteen minutes late (she did, but plenty of others at her store did, too, and none of them got fired), but because she'd been targeted after complaining about the store manager having an affair with one of the other employees. That person was receiving favorable treatment, such as better shifts and more pay than her colleagues.

Predictably, the manager denied everything. His mistress denied everything, too. The company paraded a stream of witnesses into court. They all testified under oath they'd never seen anything, never heard anything, never suspected anything. I cross-examined each one with questions that made it clear how much they liked their jobs, needed their jobs, hoped to keep their jobs. That they wanted to get promotions and raises and other benefits, and that toeing the company line wouldn't hurt those prospects, at all.

I couldn't just turn to the jury and say, "Trust me, folks, this is how they do it." I had to weave together evidence that would help lay the foundation for a closing argument where

I tied everything together. I had to show other employees had been late or had broken other rules and hadn't been fired. I had to hope the jury found my client believable and, more importantly, likable. At the end of the day, it wasn't enough for the jury to generally want to rob from the rich and give to the poor. It had to want to rob from the rich and give specifically to my poor client.

Again, that's how it goes. In every single case like this. Even if the evidence proved that the company had blatantly violated the legal rights of the employee, a jury won't give a penny to someone it just doesn't find appealing, or deserving.

Judges tell juries over and over again to not make any decisions until they hear all the evidence. But jurors start making decisions from the second the lawyers open their mouths during jury selection. Heck, jurors start making decisions from the instant they see the people sitting at either of the two tables, plaintiff and defendant and the lawyers for each side.

The jurors have to like the plaintiff, to root for her. They also have to like me, or to at least think I'm not too much of the asshole that, frankly, I am.

On one hand, I want them to think they'd want me fighting for them or their spouses or their children or their siblings or whoever they care about. On the other, if enough of them decide they don't like the client or the lawyer at some point after the trial begins, the rest of the case is a waste of everyone's time, especially mine.

No one knows whether a case has already been lost before the closing arguments begin. I had to hope enough of the jurors saw things my way. It was my job to load the believers up with the nuggets and explanations they would use to sell the case to the others. It would help to appeal straight to those jurors I thought were most likely to become the foreperson, because the opinions of the juror who gets elected team captain quite often become the opinions of the entire group.

That was my challenge on the morning of December 22. Mine and only mine. Alone on a high wire. Without a net. I had to bring it all home. To get the ones already on my side ready to enter the jury room and preach the Gospel according to John Persepio. To put enough doubt in the minds of the ones who were leaning against Sandy Matherson's cause.

I had to talk to them in plain and simple terms. No big words. No legalese. No mumbo. No jumbo.

I had to make them choose to dress up like Santa Claus for one afternoon, and to slide down the chimney with a big, fat sack of someone else's money and a tag tied to the bow that said *Sandy*.

I'd slow-played the trial just enough to nudge the closing arguments to Friday. The judge would start the day by reading pages and pages of convoluted and boring instructions to the jury. Then, I'd make the first part of my closing argument. Next, the lawyer for U-Sav-Plentee would do his entire presentation. I'd get the last word, with whatever time was left from the sixty total minutes I'd been given.

The final chunk of the closing argument would be critical. It was my last chance. I had to get them on my side. I had to get them revved up and ready to get to work on concluding that my client had been wronged. So that they'd begin crunching the numbers for her lost wages, for the emotional distress my client experienced after losing a job she'd had for more than eleven years. Then came the up-or-down, yes-or-no question of whether the mega-company with a strategically folksy lawyer should pay extra money as punishment for what it had done—and as a warning to other companies to not do the ordinary citizens of our quiet, God-fearing, law-abiding county this way.

All of these things rattled through my brain that morning as I forced myself awake after the fifth straight night of barely four hours of sleep. The shower didn't snap me out of the gray haze carved by the dull knife of fatigue. I reminded myself that I was forty-five years old. I wondered how much longer I'd be able to fight these battles on my own, against the small army of lawyers that companies like U-Sav-Plentee assigned to the cases filed against it. I loved feeling like David versus Goliath. I wondered whether it was actually Don Quixote versus windmill.

The lack of sleep pressed hard against the curves along the inside of my eyes. I blinked into the mirror to focus on getting ready. Truth-tellers have a face that's properly shaved. Truth-tellers have hair that's properly combed. Truth-tellers have a suit that properly fits. Truth-tellers have a tie that's properly tied. Truth-tellers with overactive sweat glands also wear a moisture-wicking T-shirt under the dress shirt to prevent soaked and stained armpits in the suit jacket.

It was during the drive to the office that I remembered I'd forgotten to put on the damn T-shirt. I cursed. I tried not to think about the clanking radiators in the old building, how the steam heat would combine with my stress and anxiety and a frame carrying about twenty-five more pounds than it should have. I glanced at the clock on the dashboard of the car. I didn't have time to turn around and go home to put on the T-shirt.

What I saw when I looked up made me forget all about the T-shirt.

2

CARS WHIZZED ALONG each of the four lanes connecting the suburbs to town, two moving in each direction. Three inches of snow from a week or so earlier had melted. The ground had mostly dried.

Up ahead, an old, oversized Chevy sat crooked on the shoulder. The tip of its back left corner stuck out into the right lane. A small figure in a flappy brown overcoat hunched over the open trunk. Both of his arms trembled their way toward getting whatever it was he was trying to remove.

I noticed the front end of the Chevy sinking into the gravel berm. The car had a flat tire. The man standing at the rear end of the vehicle was too old to be changing it by himself. A sigh started deep in my lungs and blew past my lips. I pulled behind the Chevy with my flashers on so that other cars would move to the left lane or at least not plow into the protruding corner of a chrome bumper attached to the kind of sharp-angled steel body the folks in Detroit hadn't made in decades.

I checked the mirrors. Another car sped by, sustained horn

blast letting both of us know the driver didn't appreciate the unexpected impediment along the path to wherever he was going. Coast now clear, I got out and headed for the old man.

He continued to fumble around inside the trunk. The lid was opened wide, looking like the unhinged mouth of a hippo.

"Having a little trouble?" I said.

"Having a lot of trouble," the old man said without turning around.

"Flat tire?"

"She blew out on me. I have a spare. I just need to get her out of here and onto there."

"Do you have triple-A or anything like that? They'll come out here and take care of you."

The old man's arms stopped moving. He steadied himself on the opening of the trunk with his right hand and turned around. He had deep grooves running down his cheeks, one on each side. Flaps of skin hung from his jaw, swollen rivers of dried wax from a squat candle that someone had forgotten to blow out before going to bed. His skull carried glasses with wide black frames. Gray eyes studied me through the haze of thick lenses. The brim of a charcoal fedora cast shadows over a nose that had one curly white hair spindling from its tip.

"Why do I need any of that when I have you?"

"I'm sorry," I told him. "I'm late. For court. I have a trial."

"What, did you get in trouble?"

I shook my head, slight grin stretching against a face that tried to resist it.

"No. I'm a lawyer."

He turned to look at my Subaru. He blew air through his nose. The wind caught a droplet of snot and threw it back against his overcoat.

"Not much of a car for a lawyer," he said.

I didn't have the time or desire for banter, even though

the old man was holding his own nicely. I started back toward the car.

"Was it something I said?" he asked.

"I'm getting my phone."

"You have a phone in your automobile?"

I turned back toward the old man, opening my mouth before deciding to just grab the phone and get this over with. I plucked it from the passenger seat and returned, scrolling through my contacts for Lou Rizzoli.

"That thing-a-ma-jig is a telephone?"

"Yes," I said without looking up at him. His confusion sparked my curiosity, but the goal at this point was to bring the interaction to an end and get to court. I could already feel the sweat starting to collect in armpits not lined with a moisture-wicking T-shirt.

I found Lou's name and pressed my thumb onto his number. I held the phone against my ear.

"I guess it is a telephone," the old man said as I waited. I grinned and nodded as politely as I could.

"Lou," I said when he answered. "I'm out here on Route 32, about a half mile from the Main Street exit. . . . There's a man with a flat tire. Can you have your cousin come out and change it for him? He can bill me. . . . It's an old Chevy. Light blue. . . . The model doesn't matter. It's the only old light blue Chevy on any stretch of Route 32 today, I can promise you that. . . . OK, thanks."

I ended the call and wrapped my fingers around the phone. Cars continued to zip past us every few seconds. Nearly all of them had moved to the left lane. I worried whether that would continue after I drove away.

"You should put your hazard lights on," I said to the man.

"It's a 1977 Impala."

"Excuse me?"

"The car. It's a Chevy Impala. 1977. Lou, that man you called, he wanted to know. You could have just asked me."

"His cousin's coming," I said. "He'll find you. But you need to get inside the car and wait. You should put your hazard lights on, so the other cars will see you here. Do you need me to help you find them?"

"I was hoping you'd help me change my tire."

"I'm sorry. I can't do that. Someone is coming."

"You're already here."

"I know. But I really have to go."

"Can't you wait with us until he gets here? Now that you mention those other cars, it would be nice to have yours back there. If someone hits it, maybe you can get something a little nicer with the insurance money."

A short burst of laughter escaped my mouth, even though I could otherwise sense my mood turning more sour as I felt the precious minutes and seconds ticking away.

"I'm sorry, but I can't. Do you need me to help you turn on your hazard lights?"

"I know where the button for my flashers is."

"OK then," I said, waiting for the man to return to the car. I went to the trunk and began to close it for him, hopeful he would catch the hint.

"You need to push it down good," he said. "It doesn't want to latch."

I put my left palm on the lid and gave it a firm shove. It snapped into place fairly easily. The old man's bushy white eyebrows raised and the corners of his mouth curled down.

"You're stronger than you look," he said.

I laughed again, and I kept waiting for him to go back to the Chevy and climb inside, or at least try to. "Do you need help getting in your car?" I said.

"I need help changing my tire."

"He'll be here soon. I promise. I have to go now. I wish I could stay."

He looked at me as I said it. "You don't mean that."

"Excuse me?"

"You said you wish you could stay," he said. "You don't mean it. Why would you say something you don't mean?"

"Really, sir, I have to go. I've tried to help. I've done everything I can. I just have to go."

"You have that telephone, you know."

"Excuse me?"

"That telephone. You called the man to tell him to have his cousin come fix the tire. You could call whoever you're supposed to go see, the judge I suppose, and tell him you're going to be a little late."

I lifted my right hand toward my face and pondered the phone. "Yeah, I could. But I don't want to. I want to be on time."

"He'd probably understand. You're being a good Samaritan."

"Sir, I am. I'm paying for someone to come out here and fix your tire."

"But you're not staying until he gets here."

At this rate, I thought, *he'll be here before I leave.*

"Like I said, I'm sorry. That part I definitely mean. You need to get in the car, put the flashers on, and wait." I turned away from him and went back toward my car.

"Do you want to see her?"

"Her who?" I said without stopping.

"My wife. She's in the car. She'll be upset that she didn't get a chance to thank you for not changing our tire."

I laughed again. "Tell her I'm sorry. And turn on those flashers. The truck will be here before you know it."

"I wish you would say hello to her. She doesn't get to see many people."

"Please tell her hello from me. And tell her I said Merry Christmas. Where are you heading, anyway?"

He smiled at me for the first time, flashing a hint of dentures that were carried just a little too loosely in his mouth.

"We're on our way home," he said.

I got inside the Subaru and watched the old man shuffle back to the Chevy. Once he finally got inside—I sort of wondered whether he was intentionally dragging his feet, just to piss me off—I turned on the engine, waited for an opening in the flow of traffic, and pulled away. I turned off my own flashers once the Subaru was clear of the Chevy. I could see in the rearview mirror two heads, sticking up barely above the dashboard. I noticed the outline of the old man's fedora.

I soon glided onto the exit ramp and began making my way through town. I drove as fast as I could under the circumstances, which included just enough other cars to require the kind of zigging and zagging I didn't want to do, not with the police station adjacent to the courthouse. I found a parking spot on the street, grabbed my briefcase from the back seat, scooped up my phone—my *telephone*—and hustled toward the main doors. I forgot, as I often did, to drop a few quarters into the parking meter.

I would have jogged and possibly even run, if I'd known the inevitable perspiration would have been sucked away from my softly jiggling upper body by the magic of modern sportswear technology. I opted for modified race-walking instead, the kind of aggressively brisk movement that possibly cries out "asshole" to anyone in the immediate vicinity who is moving at a more socially acceptable pace.

I realized a bit too late that one of the people who seemed to react to me that way was one of the jurors from my trial. I cringed when I noticed I'd potentially angered someone who would be deciding Sandy Matherson's case later that same day.

But then I wondered why that person was moving so slowly. If I was late, he was late, too. Why wasn't he in a hurry, like me?

I pulled my phone out and pressed the button to check the clock. I pushed it off and on again, to confirm the time it was showing. I tried to do the math in my head. I'd wasted at least ten minutes on the side of the road with the old man. It didn't add up.

I should have been late. Somehow, I wasn't.

3

I SAT AT the rectangular wooden table, next to Sandy Matherson. I resisted the temptation to review the twenty-seven pages of large-font notes I'd printed and three-hole punched and placed into the black binder in front of me on the mahogany surface covered with a half-inch of smoked, tempered glass. It was more important to act as if I were listening intently to the judge reciting the instructions to the jury, even though I already knew what every single word would be. I needed to nod at the right times. To steal glances in an effort to figure out which jurors were paying attention, which ones were just pretending to, and which ones seemed to be openly thinking about something else, such as everything they had to do that weekend, given that Christmas was coming on Monday.

Prior to the start of any trial, the lawyers give to the judge dueling versions of the various specific legal explanations that cover every point of law relevant to the case. After the jury hears all the evidence, the lawyers stick around in a half-lit courtroom for two or three hours and haggle over a Frankenstein monster of paragraphs and principles to be placed in logical order and read to the jury, with the expectation that any of it will truly register with them. Little of it ever does.

Plenty of judges, including the Honorable Donald T. Robertson, refuse to send a copy of the instructions with the jury as they deliberate. This raises the stakes of the closing argument. But it also gives the lawyer an extra opportunity to build credibility.

By explaining in plain and simple terms what they'd just heard, the lawyer now becomes part of the process of educating the jurors. By setting out the sometimes complex concepts in a way that makes sense and seems reasonable and believable, I could build a stack of chips that would come in handy when trying to get the jury to accept my version of the many conflicting and confusing facts they'd heard. What was important, what wasn't important. What they should listen to. What they should ignore.

I'd budgeted forty minutes to make my initial presentation. Gunther Anderson III, an older man with homespun charm and a voice not quite as deep as Sam Elliott's but every bit as mellifluous, would speak for up to an hour, if Anderson chose to use every minute of the time he had. I'd then have twenty minutes to get the last word.

I didn't like overwhelming the jury with technology. Lawyers paid by the hour love to use projectors and slickly produced video clips and computer-generated charts and graphs. I'd tell the jury this was all a way to try to distract them from the truth, of impressing them with bright, shiny objects instead of the dull, stubborn reality of cold, hard facts. For me, it was important to make a personal connection with each of the six jurors (only criminal cases use twelve), and to speak to each one of them as if I was in their living room, or as if they were in mine. Bells and whistles that interrupted this connection would make it harder to re-establish it.

That didn't mean I relied only on the words that came out of my mouth. I had a whiteboard on an easel. Old school. I'd write key words on there with a black or red marker, just two or three at a time. I'd leave them up there so they'd sink in while I talked more about them, and I'd wipe them clean when moving on to the next point I was hoping to make.

I'd also converted some of the most important documents into large cardboard posters. I would prop them onto the fold-out hooks of another easel when discussing how U-Sav-Plentee's own paperwork helped show that the company had screwed Sandy Matherson.

Proving that an employer fired a worker in violation of applicable state laws becomes a little bit of a magic trick. The lawyer representing the fired employee needs to systematically peel away every plausible reason the company has thrown at the wall for making its decision. When they're all gone, there's only one explanation left: the company actually fired the employee for an illegal reason, even though none of the company's witnesses would ever admit that.

It is not easy. The lawyer representing the company will argue it's impossible that each and every one of those fine, hard-working people got on the witness stand and committed perjury when they supported the company's side of the story. That's when I'd explain it's not about deliberately choosing to lie under oath. It's about locking into a version months before coming to trial, and sticking to it no matter what. That the lie is never made up on the witness stand. That the tall tale gets spun when the decision gets made, and from that point forward the lie keeps getting repeated and repeated and repeated until it morphs into something that feels like the truth.

Those thoughts popped around inside my brain, exploding kernels of ideas and reminders that were causing the perspiration to begin to gather along the top of my back, well before I had to stand up and perform. I knew the structure and the flow of the instructions well enough to realize the judge was nearing the end of them. His voice had become more raspy as the week went on. He mentioned at one point he'd been developing a cold. I spotted him from time to time unwrapping lozenges and discreetly popping them into his mouth. As he worked through the instructions, his voice was getting more hoarse than it had been.

He was explaining how to calculate Sandy Matherson's financial damages, if any. The other lawyer had managed to work a few extra *if anys* into the instructions, and I found myself wondering whether Judge Robertson was pausing on purpose before saying *if any* as a way to stick it to me, subtly. The campaign checks had long been cashed, and he had six years left on his term. He could get away with something that would be impossible to ever prove, something I could never accuse him of actually doing without potentially screwing up every other case of mine he'd handle. Or maybe it was just the cold he was catching. I couldn't tell, no matter how hard I tried.

I then tried even harder to push those ideas out of my brain. None of it would help me deliver the kind of closing argument I'd need in order to take advantage of the possibility that the four men and two women of the jury would be inclined to grant a tie to the runner, in the spirit of the season. Or maybe even to give Sandy the benefit of the doubt on what otherwise would have been a close call against her. Either way, it was time to roll out that red kettle and start clanging away with the bell.

"Are the lawyers prepared to make their closing arguments?"

Judge Robertson's words rumbled through what remained of his faltering voice. He seemed relieved to be finished speaking.

He'd have not much more to say, unless squabbles occurred during closing arguments. And that becomes a very high-risk proposition. If a lawyer interrupts the opponent's closing argument with an objection, the arrow had better hit the center of the target. Otherwise, it looks like the lawyer who made the objection was trying to keep the jury from hearing something extremely important to the other lawyer's presentation.

I pressed my hands against the glass top of the table. It was cool to the touch. I wished I had panels of that same glass taped against my chest, my back, and my armpits. I looked down at the binder. For the longest time, I had wanted to have enough confidence in my knowledge of a case to ignore the notes. I'd always been in awe of lawyers who could deliver their remarks without this crutch, to touch on every word that needed to be said from memory alone. I'd told myself that, one of these days, I'd be able to do it.

I don't know why or how it happened, but I decided then and there that today was one of these days. I picked up the binder, and I placed it down on my chair. I pushed the chair back under the table.

It all made me think of the time I found my dad removing the training wheels from my first bike and tossing them in the garbage can. "You know how to ride this damn thing," he'd said to me. "Now, just go ride it."

I knew I might have been making a mistake. But something pushed me forward. I'd never been much for deliberately self-destructive behavior; I preferred digging my own holes without realizing it.

It felt as if I was floating over myself, peering down at what I was doing and urging myself not to risk coming off as a babbling idiot in the most critical juncture of a case on which

I'd spent so many hours and so much money. But I couldn't stop myself. I'd left the old man and his wife alone out on the highway. I knew I shouldn't have done it. I suppose I was inflicting punishment, making myself feel the way I'd made them feel, unprotected and alone and exposed to whatever may happen next.

I could sense Judge Robertson shifting in his robe from the perch above the rest of the courtroom. I knew he was about to say something along the lines of, "Mr. Persepio, are you ready to proceed?" I also could see Sandy Matherson fidgeting in the chair next to me as she surely wondered whether she should have listened to her husband and hired the guy with the TV commercials who morphs into a poorly-generated computer animation of a Rottweiler, and then calls himself a bulldog.

I noticed the trash can nestled along the side of the table next to me, just in time. I bent down and scooped it up right as the Frosted Flakes and cup of coffee with two packs of Equal and a splash of the same two-percent milk I'd poured into the bowl of cereal escaped violently and abruptly from my stomach.

4

UPPER LIP LINED in sweat and lower lip coated in something else entirely, my mouth continued to hover over the opening to the can. I braced for a second wave. Judge Robertson instructed the bailiff to take the jury back to their room. I tried to ignore the sounds filling my ears, first the gasps and then the guffaws. They came from every direction. Opposing counsel. A smattering of onlookers. Maybe even some of the jurors. My main concern continued to be preparing for the next blast, if there was going to be one.

There wouldn't be, at least not yet. After the jury exited through the door to the right of the bench and the bailiff pushed it shut with something close to a slam, the next phase of the trial—an unexpected one—began almost instantly.

Already on his feet, Anderson started to speak, without being invited by the judge to do so.

"Your Honor, this is highly irregular," Anderson said. "Mr. Persepio clearly is not well. Under the circumstances, my only option on behalf of my clients is to request a mistrial. Without prejudice, of course."

"Mistrial?" I said, jerking my head up from the plastic tub I now hugged like Pooh with a honeypot. "He wants to pull the plug and start over? I'm fine. I'll be ready to go in a minute."

Judge Robertson tilted his head and stared at me from over his reading glasses. I finally became conscious of the fact that I had a trash can hovering under my head. A giant feedbag. In reverse.

"Mr. Persepio, you've got a little something on your chin," he rasped under flaring eyebrows.

I felt blood pulse and flow even more strongly through and across the flesh of my cheeks. Sandy Matherson, God love her, held out a napkin she'd been toting around in her purse. It smelled like cigarettes. I rubbed it over and along my jawline. I placed the trash can full of my own puke back onto the tile floor, dropping the napkin atop a mess that was already sending stray hints of a foul stink into the air.

"Thank you, Your Honor. And I truly appreciate Mr. Anderson's concern. But I'm fine."

"You didn't seem fine two minutes ago," the judge said.

"Well, yes. I know. I'm sorry. It happened. But I'm fine now."

Anderson seized the opening. "Your Honor, if I may. We can't expect the jury to focus appropriately and completely on Mr. Persepio's presentation if they are in constant fear that he might vomit on them."

"Again," I said, "I truly appreciate Mr. Anderson's concern. Although I'm not sure why he'd want the jury to be focusing appropriately and completely on my presentation. As I see it, that would help his clients, if the jury isn't listening to me. Of course, it would help his clients even more if they could avoid having this case go to a verdict three days before Christmas."

"Let's close the record for now," Judge Robertson said,

glancing at his court reporter in a signal to turn off the audio recording and to stop pressing the nondescript keys that generated a series of letters and spaces making no sense whatsoever to the untrained eye. "I'd like to see the lawyers in my chambers in twenty minutes, sharp. Mr. Persepio, I suggest you take advantage of this opportunity to get yourself some fresh air. I prefer that the receptacle in my office remain filled only with paper."

I had nothing else to say. I steadied myself against the table as Judge Robertson exited through the door directly behind his seat. I turned to Sandy Matherson, who seemed confused and horrified, but also genuinely concerned.

"Honey, are you OK?"

"I'm fine," I told her. My eyes slid to her husband. He sat in the front row of the gallery, arms crossed tightly against a red flannel shirt that had dried egg yolk or something that looked like it on the left side of the collar. "I'm fine."

Earl Matherson worked as a coal miner. I avoided his grip whenever I could, since he always seemed to save a little extra squeeze just for me, a possible reminder that he wanted Sandy to hire someone else to handle her case. Then and there, I wished she'd listened to him.

"What's happening?" Sandy said to me.

"I'm not sure. We'll talk to the judge and figure out how to proceed. They want a mistrial. That means they want to start over again, from the beginning. New jury. New everything."

"Well, I don't want to do that," she said. The twisting expression on Earl's face made it clear he didn't want to do that, either.

"That won't happen," I said. "I mean, I'm pretty sure it won't happen."

"So what's going to happen?" she said, genuinely curious and without a hint of frustration or impatience.

"I don't know," I said.

I told Sandy, loud enough for Earl to hear, that I'd take Judge Robertson's advice and get some fresh air. I didn't think I needed it, but nothing would be happening for another twenty minutes (eighteen and a half, at that point), so I decided to take a quick walk.

I opted for the steps instead of the elevator, just to get my juices (other than gastric) flowing a little bit. The staircase was wide; if I got woozy, I could just collapse sideways. Maybe just roll down to the next landing.

Fortunately for me, and for the two or three people who were climbing the stairs across from me, I didn't wipe out on the way from the third floor to ground level. I turned toward the light coming through the opening at the front of the courthouse, a deep and sweeping revolving door with traditional rectangular glass entrances on each side. I pushed my way through the spinning exit, hoping to make it outside before the security guards who might have heard about what had happened could say anything to me.

The weather continued to be far better than seasonal. Global warming or whatever, I didn't mind not having to traipse around in puddles and piles of gray slush during the final days of the calendar year.

I took a left and began to stroll down Main Street. It felt good to hear my heels clicking against the concrete. With nearly all of the storefronts long since vacated, I was mostly alone with my thoughts and the Christmas decorations lining the street, along with the tinny chimes of *Silver Bells* coming through small speakers mounted on the street lamps. I remembered being eleven years old and singing in a deliberately irritating voice "silver bells, my butt smells" in order to get a rise out of my parents, along with a laugh out of my brother.

I breathed the town's still and open air deep into my lungs. It was clean for the most part, thanks to the relative lack of cars rolling down the one-way street pointing back toward the courthouse.

I felt better already. I'd overcome whatever it was that had caused me to surrender my breakfast at an extremely inopportune moment. I wanted to get back to the courtroom, to deliver my closing argument to the jury. To get Sandy Matherson the justice she deserved. And to secure for myself the thirty-three-percent chunk of the verdict as my fee.

I checked my phone. I needed to get back to Judge Robertson's chambers in eleven minutes. I kept moving farther down the long blocks of the largely deserted downtown, happy that none of the random folks who saw me realized I'd just endured the biggest embarrassment of my professional life.

Still, I wanted to immediately face those who had seen (and heard) me throw up in open court. I wanted to get back on that horse, to commence a closing argument that would soon have them forgetting that Sandy Matherson's lawyer had puked in their presence. Maybe they'd view me heroically, like Michael Jordan in that game where he supposedly had the flu, but actually had either food poisoning or a hangover.

The fact that I already felt fine made the incident seem even more confusing. Was something wrong with me? I resolved to get a physical after the holidays. A good one, not from the guy I'd call whenever I needed a no-questions-asked prescription to be filled over the phone but a real, honest-to-goodness, needle-in-the-arm, finger-up-the-keister examination.

I reminded myself that I was fewer than five years from fifty, the birthday that provided the ultimate line of demarcation between "my God, he was so young" and "well, I guess he had a pretty full life." I think I heard a comedian say that before. I was half a decade away from not finding it very funny, at all.

I pivoted on the concrete sidewalk with eight minutes left until it was time to plead with Judge Robertson to let me continue. The wind started to blow against my face on the way back to the courthouse. It buffeted my cheeks, tickled my nose. It kept me alert and sharp.

I'd need it, especially with Anderson already pushing for a mistrial. The thought of doing this all over again from scratch would have made me nauseous, if I hadn't already rid myself of anything that could be ejected from the upper reaches of my digestive system.

I tried to clear my head as I moved, preparing for whatever might happen. Steeling myself for whatever tack I might need to take in order to persuade the judge that, no, I won't spray bits of last night's mostly digested chicken all over the front row of the jury box. I'd worked too hard to get the dimpled ball perfectly situated on the tee, and I'd already missed it and fallen down with my first swing. I had every intention to ease back into position and pound it three hundred and twenty-five yards, straight and true.

As I approached the main doors, I noticed my car parked on the street along the far side of the building. I remembered I hadn't dropped any coins in the parking meter, and I wondered whether I'd already gotten yet another ticket that would end up in the glove box until I remembered to get them all paid.

That's when I spotted a dull orange contraption that had become attached to the right front wheel. A clamp. A Denver boot. Well, screw you Colorado. This was the last thing I needed to see.

I broke into a light jog, for no real reason. The boot clung to the rim, inseparable from the structure. It was going nowhere, like that facehugging spider or whatever it was that planted the original alien that exploded out of John Hurt's stomach. Baby

Michael and I had watched that movie one night, and we both couldn't sleep right for a week.

As I got closer, I noticed another car parked crookedly in front of mine. It was the same blue Chevy from the highway.

The old man stood there, his back to the rear bumper of his car. He was studying the Subaru, for some reason. I called out to him. "Sir? Mister? I see you got your tire fixed."

He kept his eyes on the front end of my car. "I think I might have run into you a little bit when I was parking. Just a little bit."

I entered the space between the two cars, getting a little too close to the old man. It was the only way I could see what was going on. I checked the Subaru. Everything seemed to be in order. "Did you hit it?" I said. "I don't see any marks."

"I think so. I don't know. I heard a sound when I was backing up. Maybe my wife broke wind. She does that sometimes. She thinks just because she's hard of hearing I am, too."

"I think that probably sounds a little different from running into a car."

"Well, you haven't had her cooking."

I remembered that I needed to get back to Judge Robertson's chambers. I decided to worry about the bumper and the boot later. "I need to go," I said.

His eyes absorbed my face from behind the milky lenses of his glasses. "You're always in a hurry. Why is that?"

"It's a busy day. I told you before, I need to be in court."

"Why aren't you in there, then?"

"I'm on my way back in," I said. "It's a long story. But I'm glad you got your tire fixed."

"Did you see you've got something on your wheel? I don't know what that thing is. I think I have a screwdriver in the trunk. I can try to pop it off for you."

"That won't be necessary," I said, fighting off a smile. "But I do need to go."

He motioned toward the car. "Do you want to see her? I told her I saw you."

"I have to go," I said, and I started toward the front door to the courthouse. "I really am glad your tire is fixed. I thought you said you were on your way home."

"We are," he said.

I could feel him watching me as I spun around and made my way back inside.

5

I PASSED THROUGH the metal detector at the entrance to the courthouse. Two older men in burgundy jackets, white dress shirts, black slacks, and black ties saw me. They exchanged glances.

"Hey, Ralph," one said to the other, "it's Chuck."

"What's up, Chuck?" Ralph said. They both cackled.

I performed an exaggerated bow for their continued amusement. "You should have been there," I said. "It was the most memorable moment that courtroom has seen in years."

"Sounds like the best thing since the time Jerry Branson's wife found love letters from his girlfriend in the bottom of the closet," Ralph said. "Mrs. Branson showed up during trial and started whacking him against the head with an umbrella, while he was questioning a witness. I was the bailiff then. I seen it happen."

"What did you do?" I said.

"I enjoyed the show. I figured if I tried to get in the middle of that, she'd start whacking me, too."

"I bet old Reggie didn't try to get between your face and that trash can today," said the other guard, whose name was either Paul or Phil. I could never remember which one it was, and it was far too late to ask.

"Will you be starting up again?" Ralph said.

"I'm about to find out. We're meeting with the judge. I need to get up there."

I started for the steps back to the courtroom. Ralph called out to me. "Hey!" he said, waiting until I had twisted back in their direction. "Bye, Chuck." Their raucous laughter echoed into the entrance to the stairwell.

I checked my phone, expecting to be right on time or maybe even a minute or two behind schedule. It showed I was five minutes early. I shook my head and dropped the thing back in my pocket.

Once on the third floor, I made my way through the hallway leading to the entrance to Judge Robertson's private office. Anderson stood there, tugging with his hands at the lapels of a tailored suit that was expensive enough to not seem expensive at all.

"Feeling better, Counselor?" Anderson said.

"I'm fine," I said. "I've been fine. It was a fluke thing."

"Fluke things happen. When you've done this as long as I have, you see everything. After today, I guess I can now say I truly have seen it all."

"I'm glad I could help you finish up your bucket list," I said.

"Well, I'm not the one who needed the bucket today."

I held my tongue, because I didn't have a particularly good response. Which meant there was a decent chance my next comment would have included a profane remark or two. The last thing I needed after puking in court was to start an obscenity-laced shouting match with the opposing lawyer at the edge of Judge Robertson's chambers, three days before Christmas.

"Should we let him know we're ready?" I said.

"He stepped out. I saw him go. He said something about running down to get the title renewed on his truck, since he had a few unexpected minutes."

I tried not to let myself get paranoid over whatever else Anderson and Judge Robertson might have discussed. The rules prohibit direct communications between the judge and one of the lawyers about any case. But what would have stopped Judge Robertson from making a sarcastic remark about my performance that morning? Even if it had nothing to do with the actual trial itself, the thought of becoming a shared punchline among my peers made me feel queasy all over again.

We heard Judge Robertson approaching before we saw him. He was talking on his phone, giving someone instructions with that raspy voice about where to be and what to bring for whatever it was he'd be hosting that night, maybe a Christmas party. If so, my family's contributions to his campaigns weren't sufficiently exorbitant to secure an invitation.

Not that we would have gone. Linda had cajoled me into having a party of our own that night. I'd forgotten all about it. I wished I hadn't remembered.

"Gentlemen," Judge Robertson said, nodding once in the general direction of both of us. "Follow me."

He led the way. Anderson followed. I stopped at the threshold, holding the doorknob. "Would you like me to close this?" I asked.

"Ordinarily, yes," the judge said, "but if you think you'll be making a mad dash to the bathroom, perhaps we should leave it open."

My eyes shot toward Anderson, who didn't make a sound but who had a self-satisfied grin pushing the thickened flesh of late middle age away from the corners of his mouth.

"I guess I'll leave it open, just in case," I said.

Judge Robertson walked behind a large desk, full of impeccably polished dark wood. Not a scuff or a smudge could be seen anywhere on it. He had piles of paper in different heights neatly stacked on the surface, six or seven of them. I assumed each corresponded to one of his most active cases. He sat down. The lawyers continued to stand.

"Take a load off," he said, motioning to a long table in his office with several chairs positioned around it. The largest of the seats pressed snugly into the space under one end. Anderson and I both knew that one belonged to the judge, regardless of whether he currently chose to use it.

I took a spot on the side closest to Anderson and me. He moseyed toward the other, easing his imported suit that looked not-imported into a space directly across from where I sat. At least if I threw up again, it would be aimed right at him.

"Your honor," Anderson said, once again leveraging his age and experience to speak without express invitation to do so, "I must renew my request for a mistrial. This is highly unusual. Mr. Persepio is clearly not feeling well. And given the looming holidays, the idea of having these jurors set the evidence and the instructions aside for two weeks and then start up again after the first of the year would be unfairly prejudicial to my clients."

"I don't know how many different ways I have to say I'm fine," I said, speaking directly to Anderson. "It's been a half hour. We can start the closings, take a lunch break, and the jury can deliberate after that."

"What if they haven't reached a decision by five o'clock?" Anderson said, ignoring me and directing his words to the judge. "When would they return? The day after Christmas? The day after that? They should be allowed to enjoy their holiday without the burdens of unresolved legal business."

"He has a point, Mr. Persepio," the judge said. "I never know how long a jury will be out in any of these cases. I was already a little nervous about giving it to them this morning. And it's not fair to either side if they rush to a decision because they want to put this behind them. I thought they'd start deliberating yesterday afternoon. If I recall correctly, Mr. Persepio, you told me on Monday you fully expected that to be the situation."

"It was," I said. "I mean, I did. I thought that would happen." The implication of his remarks put me on the defensive, especially since it was accurate. Without thinking, I blurted out a lie. "I didn't want them to get it today."

"Of course you did," Anderson said. "You were hoping for an early Christmas gift from the jury. We're all adults, John. We know what you were trying to do."

"Well, if you'd handle the scheduling conferences for your cases directly and not assign someone fresh out of law school to grind the file while you're off golfing with Senator Jacobson, this week wouldn't have been picked for the trial."

"That'll be fine, Mr. Persepio," Judge Robertson said. "I know how demanding trial can be, especially when you're practicing alone. No sleep. Constant activity. It's exhausting. It's stressful. But I still expect the lawyers to treat each other with respect, no matter how out of sorts they might be feeling."

"I apologize, Your Honor," I said. "For everything. Yes, I wanted to try the case this week. Who wouldn't? And we did. And the jury is here and we're here. And we should go ahead and finish this up right now."

"And I renew my motion for a mistrial," Anderson said, "without prejudice."

Anderson and I glared at each other, neither saying another word. Judge Robertson remained silent, pensive. I was holding my breath without realizing I was holding my breath. That's all I needed. To hyperventilate and then get sick all over again.

"Here's what we're doing," Judge Robertson said. "We'll reconvene on Tuesday, January 2. I'll read the instructions again, and then you'll make your closing arguments."

"What?" I blurted out with a tone that was involuntarily petulant. "Are you joking? You seriously expect these people to remember all of this eleven days from now?"

"Mr. Persepio, I'd prefer not to commence the proceedings on the second of January with a contempt hearing. You'll agree with me on that?"

"I'm sorry," I said, sensing the smugness ooze from the pores on Anderson's oversized nose. "I note my objection."

"We'll do this on the record in the courtroom," the judge said, "and you can note your objection there. If you hope to pursue an appeal because I pulled the plug for a week and a half after you expelled into a trash can at the outset of closing arguments, well, I suspect the parties' legal briefs will provide me with a certain degree of entertainment value."

I had nothing more to say, lest I actually end up in jail for Christmas morning. Anderson had nothing to say for different reasons. He hadn't gotten what he'd asked for, but he probably asked for a mistrial in the hopes of getting exactly what he got.

The judge stood and motioned for us to do the same. "Let's bring the jury back in and I'll explain it to them," the judge said. "Then we can send everyone home for the holidays."

Anderson and I pushed out of our seats as well. He started for the open door. I waited for him to move toward the exit before following. I heard someone talking to me in a low voice. It was the judge.

"Mr. Persepio," he said, "are you sure you're OK?"

"I feel fine, why?"

"During the break, I was downstairs. I saw you out on the street, by your car."

"The boot," I said. "I've had some parking tickets. I need to get them paid."

"Not that. It looked like you were—I don't know how to put it—talking to yourself."

"There was another man out there, next to me. He'd backed his car into my bumper. We were checking for any damage."

"Well," Judge Roberston said, "I didn't notice any other man. And I definitely didn't notice any other car."

6

I COULDN'T TELL whether the jury received the news with relief or disappointment. Sandy Matherson wasn't happy to learn she wouldn't be having her own December to remember, but she stifled her reaction, since both she and I knew Earl would be pissed enough for both of them. I talked to her about the situation after the bailiff had once again led the jury out of the courtroom so that they could start their very extended break in the trial.

Earl's face had already developed a shade of red that nearly matched his flannel shirt. He pressed his forearms so hard against his torso that with one good squeeze his head would have been launched into low orbit.

I fiddled with the contents of one of the boxes of paperwork that would stay in the courtroom until we resumed. The judge had said no other business would be conducted there during the week of Christmas, so we could leave everything where it was. I moved slowly while pretending to organize the files in the hopes that Sandy and Earl would go. They didn't.

Meanwhile, Anderson and his minions had packed up the gadgets they planned to use during their presentation and embarked on a long weekend that wouldn't entail licking six-, seven-, or maybe even eight-figure wounds. I tried not to think about the possibility of a verdict that large, especially since it would have been tied up for months on appeal. Still, having a major award tied up on appeal is a lot better than not having one.

Soon, three people remained in the courtroom: Sandy, Earl, and me. Sandy checked once more to her left and to her right to confirm we were alone. She nevertheless whispered.

"Was there any talk in there about, you know, settling this?"

"Nothing more than before," I said. "They've been pretty firm in their position. It makes it a lot easier to go forward when we know we don't have that bird in the hand."

"What was it before?" She knew the answer. I could tell she wanted me to say it in front of Earl, that maybe he didn't believe her.

"They offered ten thousand dollars before trial," I said. "That's nothing. It's peanuts. It wouldn't even cover my costs."

"Now, what does that mean?" Again, she already knew the answer to the question. Maybe if we won she should go to law school. After first going to college. She was definitely sharp enough to do it, if Earl would simply allow her to.

"I've paid for everything so far. I get that money back from whatever we recover. That's money I've paid out of pocket, money that's not coming back if we lose."

"And we don't pay you that if we don't win, right? Because that's not what that letter you sent says."

"I know," I said, eyeing Earl carefully since he was actually the one asking these questions. "Technically, I can't say in advance that you won't owe me the money. But if we get nothing, I'm not going to ask you for a dime. I took this case to try to make things better for you. The last thing I'm going to do is make things worse."

That's when Earl could no longer help himself, even though he'd likely been told by his wife to not say anything to me. "You sure ain't made nothing better yet," he said. "You said we was getting an answer on this today. We expected an answer on all of this before Christmas. Now that there judge is saying we gotta come back after New Year's Day? Well, that sure don't seem fair to me."

"I don't disagree with you, Earl."

"The way I see it, you're the one that's supposed to keep unfair shit from happening to my wife."

Sandy's eyes flashed at him. "Earl, he's trying the best he can."

"Well, then he should have been trying not to puke all over himself."

I tried my best to stay calm. I wanted to lash out at anyone and anything over what had happened that morning. I had real skin in the game, just like they did. More than they did. I'd spent more money than I wanted to calculate chasing U-Sav-Plentee on this one, and it was as good of a case as I was ever going to take to trial against a company that big.

The truly strong claims settle, because the company's lawyers don't want to have their names attached to a massive verdict. So they make the plaintiffs an offer they can't refuse. To get the planets to line up just right for a runaway jury, the company and the lawyers had to think they had a clear winner. Most of the time, they did. Once in a while, they found out the hard way they didn't.

The best thing going for Sandy, Earl, and me in this case was that we wanted the jury to take what would amount to pocket change from a beast that swallowed up money on money on money, especially when their stores were at maximum earning capacity during the holidays. Already that morning, three days before Christmas, U-Sav-Plentee's worldwide operations likely had cleared in profit more than a hundred times the amount we would have won, even if I'd been allowed to ply the jury with tequila and cocaine during their deliberations.

My ace in the hole, the proximity of the deliberations to Christmas Day, would dissolve into dust by January 2. And it had happened because, for whatever reason, I had a rapid bout of nausea that had resolved itself faster than I could even realize it was happening.

"Folks, I'm sorry about this. I've said all along we have to play the hand we've been dealt. That's really all we can do at this point."

"Why don't you call that other lawyer and see if they want to settle?" Earl said. "He sure seems smart."

I was smart enough to pick up on the message. I kept fighting to not take the bait. "That won't work at this point. They'll sense weakness. They'll refuse. If they didn't do it before this morning, they're definitely not going to do it before we come back."

"Well, I hope you and your family have a nice Christmas," Earl replied. "And I hope you'll be thinking about the kind of Christmas my family will have because of this."

Sandy continued to glare at him. The fact that she hadn't stopped him told me, deep down, she felt the same way. It also told me, no matter how many times I'd explained it in plain terms to Sandy, they didn't fully realize they wouldn't have been presented with a giant ceremonial check by the CEO of U-Sav-Plentee that same day, if we'd won.

"I ain't asked you for nothing through all of this," he said.

"But I'm asking for one thing. And I ain't really asking. I want you to come to our house on Tuesday. I want you to pretend I'm that jury. I want you to tell me exactly what you would've said to convince them to make this right, if you would've got up there and done it today."

That was the last thing I wanted to do, the last thing I planned to do. At that point, however, I just wanted to get out of there. So I agreed to do it. I'd figure out later how to get out of it. Not that I'd have a lot of time in the coming weekend to devise a plan that would have a chance of working.

I told them, given Earl's request, I needed to gather a few things to bring with me on Tuesday, which prompted them to finally make their exit. After they did, I went back to the table, pulled out the chair, and sat in it for a long time, staring at the seats where the jurors had been sitting all week. Ready to hear my closing argument. Perhaps ready to change Sandy's life and mine, just by writing a number in a box on a sheet of white paper. And now, just like that, the moment was gone forever.

Ho ho ho. Merry Freaking Christmas.

7

AFTER I FINISHED feeling sorry for myself, or whatever I was doing in that seat for so long, I pulled the phone out of my pocket. I'd placed it on do not disturb. A few calls had come from the office. Curiosity undoubtedly was getting the better of Barb, who served as my receptionist and paralegal and whatever else was needed to help me with the constant plate-spinning of a one-lawyer practice.

I didn't feel like explaining to her what had happened. But I at least had to let her know the trial wouldn't be finished until after the holidays. I decided to tell her by text message that the case had been delayed until January 2.

I didn't offer an explanation. She didn't ask for one. That told me she'd likely heard all about it from someone she knew at the courthouse. Regardless, I'd already given her the full week of Christmas off. By the time she returned, I'd be back in court trying to clean up the mess that literally lingered in the bin to my left.

I had a stream of texts from Linda, too. At some point, I'd have to tell her about the unexpected misadventures that had squandered my supposedly golden opportunity, and that had been reduced to whatever was still gurgling on the floor beside me. I definitely didn't feel like explaining to her any of what had happened, since the news would have been met with a machine gun of questions flowing from the thinly-veiled premise of "I told you so."

At least I wouldn't get any second-guessing about why I'd taken the case in the first place or how I'd gone about trying to gather evidence or why I didn't dump so-and-so from the jury or why I did or didn't say or do whatever I had or hadn't said or done in court that had led to the result. This would be more along the lines of "you need more sleep" or "you should get more exercise" or "you eat too fast" or "you eat too much" or "why didn't you check the date on the milk?" or "why didn't you excuse yourself?" or "why didn't you convince the judge to let you keep going?" I'd bristle at the inquisition, she'd say she was just trying to help, and I'd reply that there was nothing actually helpful about any of it.

I remembered again that she'd insisted on having the party that night.

It was my own fault for not getting her to do it on a different day, or to not do it at all. But I'd allowed myself to get caught up in the all-in bet I'd made, by the confidence/ delusion it would fall together just right, that the Spirit of Christmas would intervene and give us the kind of outcome I'd been chasing for years, battling through the infield singles and ground-rule doubles, all in the hopes of eventually circling the bases triumphantly after hitting a walk-off grand slam.

Facing Linda, Barb, and anyone else would have been much easier if I'd just lost the damn case. That had already happened to me, more than a few times. Any lawyer who boasted about never losing at trial hadn't tried many cases, because the best that ever can be hoped for when a trial actually makes it all the way to verdict is a fifty-fifty track record.

Too much changes from the time it all begins until the jury completes the verdict form and knocks loudly on that door. It was a sound that used to fill me with wonder but now mostly conjured only dread, no matter the outcome. Still, win some or lose some, not many lawyers can claim they managed to turn a potentially huge victory into an inevitable failure because they'd thrown up in front of the jury as they were getting ready to deliver a closing argument.

Linda also would insist I get checked out. That's something I already planned to do. The fact that she would push me to do it would make me not want to. It was stupid, it was juvenile. But if I hadn't changed by the time I was halfway to ninety years old, when was I ever going to?

I noticed at the bottom of Linda's messages a request to stop on my way home from court and get some things she needed for the party. As if I'd want to interrupt my euphoria or emerge from my despair to push a cart up and down and around the aisles of a grocery store. Fortunately, the purgatory into which I'd plunged put me in the right frame of mind to want to accomplish something tangible, even if it was as simple as making sure I got everything on a list of items ranging from four types of soda to a large package of paper towels (not the cheap ones) to long-nose lighters for igniting the wicks of the red and green candles that littered the first floor of the house to three boxes of different kinds of crackers to a tray featuring processed meats and cheeses that the mother of one of my former clients (I'd gotten him a good settlement, so she didn't hate me) slapped together on a Styrofoam rectangle and covered snugly in plastic wrap.

I responded with a simple OK to Linda's request and deferred any further discussion until later. Hopefully, until much later.

Then there was the matter of the large iron clamp plastered to the wheel of my car. I managed to slink out of the courthouse largely unnoticed (I got a hearty "Merry Christmas, Chuck!" from Ralph as I sped through the revolving door), and I stopped at the car to collect the various unpaid tickets from the glove compartment. I plucked the newest one from beneath the wiper.

I headed for the city building, two blocks away from the county courthouse. I suffered through the slurred attitude of Doris Evans, who'd been enjoying her last workday of the year with a little Christmas cheer, one of the privileges of holding a job for more than thirty orbits around the sun and having a much younger supervisor who was physically, mentally, and emotionally afraid of her. For most people, a little nip or two made them happier. Doris, in that regard and many others, wasn't most people.

She huffed at having to do some work on the final workday before Christmas, to count up the amount I owed and to calculate the interest. She actually asked to see my driver's license so that she could take down the information, as if I were going to settle up my debt by passing a bad check.

She said there might not be anyone available to remove the boot until the following week. I reminded her if someone had been on duty that day to apply the thing, there surely was someone on duty that day to take it off. She narrowed her right eye into a look that conveyed the two-word message she was not yet tipsy enough to say out loud without fear of discipline, even for her.

I smiled at her restraint, and I waited until I saw her make the call and heard her convey the order to remove the boot from a white Subaru with the numbers from my license plate. I nodded to her, thanked her far too effusively for it to be genuine, and called out loudly into the otherwise empty room, "Merry Christmas to all, and to all a good night!"

I didn't rush back to the car, assuming the guy whom Doris had phoned would take his sweet time in taking off the boot. To my surprise, a man in a city-issued gray work uniform was hunched by the wheel, unlocking the face of the immobilizer and scooping it from the ground. I didn't recognize him, but he seemed to know me.

"Well, well," he said. "It's Mr. Lawyer."

"Thanks for doing this so quickly."

"Not a problem, Mr. Lawyer. I wanted to be sure you could get home. I heard you had a big day."

"Excuse me?"

"Gary Galloway is my brother-in-law," the man said, swinging the clamp into the bed of a white pickup truck littered with dents and chips and other imperfections reflecting the reality that no one who ever drove it owned it. "You know, he's the guy you sued when you sued his company."

"Sorry, pal," I said. "We all have a job to do." It was a small town; awkward exchanges like that happened from time to time. I didn't feel like explaining to this guy what he already should have known—I didn't sue his brother-in-law in order to get money from him but because I needed a resident of the state to be named as a defendant in order to keep the case from getting sucked into federal court, where it would have been much, much harder to win. (Like I said before, I know how that sounds. Like I also said before, that's how it always works.)

The guy slammed the tailgate shut before turning back to me. He crossed his arms and leaned against it. "My sister is worried sick about this. She may leave him over it."

"It would be that way even if I didn't sue him personally," I said, moving to inspect the wheel before getting in the car. "It's just the way it is."

The guy's casual demeanor didn't match his words or his tone. He probably suspected a courthouse security camera attached to a building or a light pole was capturing our movements.

"People like you play games with other people's lives," he said.

"Actually, I try to help improve things for people whose lives have been played games with."

"That don't make no sense."

I matched his body language. It was sort of fun to trade verbal hostilities without getting in someone's face, and more importantly without having someone get in mine.

"Your brother-in-law was sleeping with one of his employees," I said. "My client found out about it. She complained. Then they fired her for it."

"That's not how I hear it."

I stepped toward him, curious to see whether he'd do the same. I had an urge to invite a punch in the face, if it meant he'd be fired. After considering how a black eye or a broken nose would look in the Christmas pictures, I instead crossed the front of the Subaru and leaned over to open the door on the driver's side.

"Of course that's not how you hear it," I said.

He pushed himself from the truck and put his hands on his hips. "The company's lawyer says you filed a frivolous lawsuit."

"Do you know what a frivolous lawsuit is?" I said. "It's every lawsuit filed against the person who calls it frivolous."

"Well," he said as he climbed into the truck, "you'll find out just how frivolous this one is when that jury makes its decision. I just hope my sister can hold up. It would be a real shame if she couldn't. It would be a real shame if someone had to do something about that."

He slammed the door and drove away, giving the accelerator a hard push so that the truck belched a dark cloud of exhaust in my direction. The smoke lingered amid the fumes of the vague threat he'd just made. It wasn't the first time someone had made a comment like that to me, but I'd never had any actual problems. It probably was just a matter of time before something like that happened. For now, I had plenty of other things to worry about.

It didn't stop me from giving him the finger as the truck rolled away.

I THOUGHT ABOUT stopping at the Super U-Sav-Plentee on my way home to buy most of the items from Linda's list. I'd rarely set foot in there since I started representing former employees of the company's local mega-store. Some of the workers regarded me as a hero. Most of them, swallowing the Kool-Aid so many of the managers and co-managers and assistant managers had an active role in mixing up and scooping out, loathed me. I didn't care. The naysayers would change their tune abruptly, if they ever got fired. Plenty of them had, plenty more surely would.

I tried to force myself to whistle a Christmas song as I lugged my two-sizes-too-big frame from the Subaru to the sliding doors of the grocery store where I had no known friends or foes, other than my former client's mother who worked in the deli. (The workers there were unionized; if anyone got fired, they couldn't sue the company in court.) I couldn't settle on one specific tune. I started with three or four notes of

Jingle Bells followed by a few bars of *Rudolph* before it all melted into *You're a Mean One, Mr. Grinch.*

The automatic glass doors slid open with a familiar hiss. I walked inside. The activity within the corrugated-steel box created a level of noise much greater than it was during my usual visits. The clamor of everything happening, from harried, happy people talking to other happy, harried people to carts rolling toward their destinations to grocery baggers bagging groceries, drowned out the holiday music leaking from speakers in the ceiling tiles. That was good, because I could hear just enough to know it was some post-modern bubble-gum bastardization of a classic that was perfectly fine when it was coming from the vocal cords of someone like Perry Como.

I started toward the collection of steel cages on rickety wheels. I stood, patiently as I could, while customers who were oblivious to the fact that others might need to get a cart of their own took their sweet time removing, twisting, and pushing away. Given that it was so close to Christmas, I tried not to roll my eyes too conspicuously or to sigh too loudly. I might not have succeeded.

I waited for an opening to grab a cart and get started. Too many people were taking up too much space. I tried to tell myself it was fine. The longer I spent at the store, the longer it would be before I would possibly have to share with Linda a story I never dreamed I'd tell, and she surely never dreamed she'd hear.

As some of the other customers moved away, I noticed a man struggling to pull a cart from the rest of them. I recognized the size, the shape, the coat. The fedora. Even before he turned, I knew it was him. Again.

I yanked one free for him, ripping it away with a grunt.

"They can be a little stubborn," he said, showing no surprise at running into me for the third time that day. "I was wondering when you'd get here."

I doubted whether I'd heard what I thought I heard, but I didn't want to get into a discussion with him over whether he'd said what I thought he said. "My wife wants me to pick up some things for tonight," I explained.

"Sounds like someone is having a party," he said as he fought to twist his cart in the direction he hoped to eventually guide it. I gave it a nudge with my hip to get it moving.

"Someone is having a party. But not me. My wife. For her colleagues. I'm just there to make sure everything works out."

"An innocent bystander," the old man said, "who'd rather be standing by innocently elsewhere."

I laughed not only at the turn of phrase but at the accuracy of the observation. It was the last place I wanted to be that night. It was the only place I could go. Long gone were the days of heading to a bar and getting a few beers with the guys. At this point in my life, I wouldn't even know where to find the right place. I also wasn't sure who the guys would be. Every adult male I knew had a wife and a family and would be spending their time with them two nights before Christmas Eve, or at Linda's party.

"Do you shop here regularly?" I said to the old man, following him as he kept struggling to keep the cart moving the right way.

"I'm not shopping. I know what I need."

"Isn't that the same thing?"

"People who shop don't know what they're looking for," he said. "I know exactly what I'm looking for."

"Do you have your list?"

He stopped and turned toward me. A crooked index finger with a nail that could use a trimming tapped against the side of his head. "It's all in here."

I held up my phone. "I'm not that lucky. I've got mine right here."

"Your telephone?" the old man said. "You're going to call someone and they're going to tell you what to buy?"

"No. It does more than—never mind. Yes, I'm going to call someone. My wife."

"You should have called your wife more often."

"Excuse me?"

"Did you not understand what I said?"

"I do, I just think it's a little, well, it's a strange thing to say," I said. "And it's a strange way to say it."

"What's strange is for a man to not call his wife as much as he should."

I twisted my neck to the left and right, searching for the camera crew that was about to tell me I'd been the victim of some sort of all-day practical joke. "I'm going to get my things," I said to the man, working past the slow shuffling that barely moved his cart toward the produce section at the front of the store. I stopped and turned back to him. "By the way, I thought you said you were on your way home."

"We are," he said, with a smile softly brightening a face complicated by wrinkles and dominated by two rectangular slats of blurred prescription glass. "We're on our way home."

"Well, travel safely," I said with a nod.

I turned my attention to collecting the items from Linda's list. I heard the old man say one more thing to me. "Do you want to see her? She asked about you again."

I felt my shoulders slump with guilt, not for anything I'd done but for what I was about to do. I pivoted again. I stared at the cloudy lenses covering his eyes. "You've asked me that three times now. I haven't said yes once. That probably tells you something."

"I suppose it tells me you don't want to see her."

"It's nothing personal," I said. "I've got a lot going on. It hasn't been a good day, and it's not getting any better. So, again, give her my regards. I'm sure you're a lovely couple. I wish you nothing but the best. I hope you have a Merry Christmas."

"Until we meet again," he said as I moved forward with determination to the deli, for the finest selection of meats and cheeses money could buy in a place that wasn't an actual deli.

I thought I heard him faintly repeat himself, but I wasn't sure and didn't stop to listen.

"Until we meet again."

I forced away, as best I could, any lingering thoughts of the old man and his wife who wanted to meet me. I had things of my own to buy (not shop for, apparently), and I hoped to time my return to the house so that Linda would be distracted just enough with party preparations to not grill me the way she ordinarily would about what had happened in court. Maybe, if I got lucky, I could delay it all the way through and beyond Christmas Day. Maybe I could manage to fend off the firing squad of doubt-riddled questions until after the trial resumed and I inevitably lost.

I made my way up and down the aisles, bracing myself from time to time for yet another encounter with the old man. Maybe he'd have a bad wheel on his cart, or maybe he'd need me to get something he couldn't reach from the top shelf. Or maybe he'd pester me again about meeting his wife.

I didn't see him. I couldn't tell whether I wanted to. I sort of did. There was a strange comfort in those exchanges, probably because they had become the lone constant during one of the most upside-down days I'd experienced in years.

I checked the list on the phone, ensuring I'd gotten everything that Linda had included in her various messages. Once I thought I had it all, I made my way to one of the checkout lines. I loaded everything onto the conveyor belt, crammed a plastic card into the square machine, punched the numbers, thanked the cashier and the bagger, and began wheeling the cart toward the car.

As I approached the Subaru, my eyes scanned the parking lot for the old Chevy. Its size and age would have made it stand out. If it was there, I didn't see it. As much as I didn't want to ever see that car again, part of me wanted to.

It distracted me just enough to keep me from realizing I'd forgotten to grab a large package of paper towels.

9

FROM THE INSTANT the metal door landed on the concrete pad in the garage, I found myself fighting the urge to be anywhere else. I wasn't proud of the feeling, but I couldn't help how I felt.

I could hear Joseph yelling at Mark. I could hear Mark shouting at Macy. I could hear the dog barking at the commotion. As soon as I opened the door into the house the cat would make his escape from it all, bolting past me and finding the familiar empty corner in back of the second row of the metal shelves screwed into the cinderblock wall, next to a box of old football cards I'd saved for my sons if they ever showed any interest in them. They never did. Maybe Macy would.

I hollered for help with the groceries. Not that I had very many. But I had this thing about them not getting soft, so I put the boys to work whenever I could. It could be one of the reasons why they didn't seem to have much use for me, except when they wanted something.

Only Macy arrived at the door, gazing up from behind black frames containing thick, clear slabs that corrected extreme nearsightedness. I thought it looked ridiculous for a five-year-old to wear Coke-bottle lenses, but Linda said Macy was too young for contacts. I told Linda that Macy wasn't too young to forever be stigmatized as the kid with the goofy-ass glasses.

"Hi Daddy. Can I help you with the bagsth? I want to make sure I sthtay on the nicthe listht."

I looked at her, not obsessing for a change over the lisp I'd repeatedly told Linda we needed to get fixed before the other kids pounced on that, too. I focused on her glasses. They reminded me of the old man.

"Earth to Daddy," she said.

"Sure," I said. "Where are your brothers?"

"I can do it," she said, breezing past me and heading for the trunk of the Subaru. The curled pieces of light brown hair running around the back of her head bounced as she moved. "If they're on the naughty listht, more for me. Didn't you sthay that'sth how it worksth?"

"What's that, honey?"

She turned, throwing a tiny little fist against each hip. "You sthaid that in a housthe with more than one kid, if one is nic-the and the restht are naughty, the one who's nicthe gets more to make up for the ones who are naughty."

"That's right, Macy," I said, letting her lead me to the back of the car. She popped the button, pushed up the lid, and inspected the contents.

"Not too much here," she said. "I'll take these." She picked up one bag in each hand and began making her way inside.

I leaned over the trunk. It dawned on me that I'd forgotten the paper towels. I cursed.

"I heard that," Macy said, pleased with herself. "That'sth a dollar for the sthwear jar."

I lifted the other bags, pushing the thin, flimsy plastic handles up my right arm in order to get as much as I could without making a second trip. I scooped the rest of them with my left hand and used my elbow to shove the trunk shut.

Joseph and Mark started up again as soon as I entered the house. I noticed only slightly less clutter than what I'd stepped over and around that morning. "You kids need to be cleaning up," I called out to no one in particular. "Your mother can't do everything."

"And your father can't do anything." Linda's voice came from the left, in the kitchen where she worked on the last of the cookies for the party. The smell gave me a moment of comfort, one that was gone as fast as it had arrived. "Weren't you going to add that part?"

"I stopped at the store. And I'm home. Whatever you need me to do, I'll do."

"After you sleep for the next three hours."

"What's that old song? I'll sleep when I'm dead?"

"You and me both," she said. She had oven mitts on each hand. Trays of sugar cookies that Macy would clamor to help *frostht* were cooling. Linda's hair, still a rich and natural auburn, was pulled up in a bun, keeping it out of the way. A few random strands had escaped.

She looked great, and I was starting to look like I should be living under a bridge. She'd still spend more time than necessary getting herself ready for the party. Really, she didn't seem much different than when we'd met in college.

Three kids later, she still had her figure and I was the one carrying the baby weight. That's what happens when they don't finish their chicken nuggets and fries at the fast-food shop masquerading as an actual restaurant and their dad decides to have one or two or as the case may be every last morsel they didn't eat, munching through the echoes of the relentless message from childhood that no scrap of food should ever be wasted.

"I got everything you wanted," I said, raising my arms to display the bags in addition to the ones Macy had dropped onto the marble island top before skittering away to whatever had caught her attention. "But I forgot the paper towels."

"Then you didn't get everything I wanted," she said, without turning her face toward me.

"I can go back."

"It's fine," she said. "I'll have Kathy bring some."

"No, I'll go."

She finally spun around. "I said it's fine."

"And I said I'll go. I just forgot. I don't mind going back. It's my fault."

"We've got four rolls. For now, at least. With the kids, four rolls can quickly become no rolls."

I could sense she was frustrated. She probably thought I wasn't paying close enough attention to the list, or whatever. I wasn't, but at least I had a decent reason. I preferred to avoid addressing it, of course. Maybe it was good that I forgot the paper towels. I'd rather she be disappointed in me for forgetting the paper towels than for doing in open court one of the things paper towels are used to clean up. I placed the other bags on top of the island and began removing the items without saying anything else.

"How'd it go today?" she eventually said. "I don't see a bottle of champagne in those bags. Maybe that's the answer."

"You seem to be awfully calm about the possibility I had my rear end handed to me."

"I don't really have the luxury of worrying about it right now. I've got a lot more to do before tonight."

Next came another one of those lapses, when the filter between my brain and my vocal cords betrayed me. Actually, they happened far too often to count as lapses. "You're the one who had to do this tonight, not me," I said.

Her green eyes flashed in my direction. "Really?" she said. "That's where you're going? You had plenty of chances to tell me not to do this tonight. I asked you fifty times. You said, every single time, it's fine. Go ahead. It's fine."

"I wasn't really thinking."

"That's the problem, John. You're never really thinking. You're never really paying attention. You're so caught up in everything but what's going on around here."

"Well, you know, it's not like I'm not occupied by things aimed at helping to pump more money into what's going on around here."

She threw off the oven mitts, looking like a hockey player spoiling for a bare-knuckled brawl. "Here we go again. That's your excuse for everything. You're trying to make more money. More money. More money. How much money did you make this year, John?"

"I don't know," I said. "Enough."

"Enough isn't good enough. I know enough about those cases you take. You love chasing ghosts. You believe whatever bullshit those people feed you when they're looking for a lawyer."

Macy's voice shot into the kitchen. "Sthwear jar!"

"I'm trying to help those people get justice," I said.

"Please," Linda said, waving a hand carrying the diamond ring I'd given her on the same day I'd received my law school diploma. "You get so drunk on the possibility of getting a huge verdict that you lose sight of whether your clients actually deserve it. Most of them got what they should have gotten, John. Haven't you ever realized that? These companies don't fire the employees they value. They get rid of the ones who shouldn't be there. They're not stupid."

"That's not how it works. You know that."

"I know that in some years you barely make enough to keep the bills paid at your office," she said as she pulled from the refrigerator two cans of frosting. "And that if I wasn't working, we'd have trouble keeping the bills paid here."

"That's not fair. I make more money than you do."

"Not per hour. I work seven hours a day at school and then I'm home. I'm home at night. I'm home on the weekends. I'm home all summer. I do everything here because you're constantly pursuing what you call justice for people who just want cash. You're trying to win the lottery, and you keep buying one shitty ticket after another."

"Sthwear! Jar!"

I became keenly aware that everyone in the house was listening to this. Macy, Joseph, Mark. The dog. Everyone but the cat, whose presence in his safe space in the garage proved he was the most evolved organism on the premises.

"I can only take the cases that come my way."

"Maybe you should do a better job of getting cases. Did you hear about the settlement Frank Williams got last week from that truck crash out on Route 32? Why can't you get a case like that?"

"Because I don't want to put my name and my face on those stupid commercials he does."

"Those stupid commercials are making him the kind of money you keep trying to make."

"Just let me do it my way. My way is working."

"It's not working well enough. If it was, you would have bought a bottle of champagne at the store. Or maybe six of them."

"The case isn't over yet," I said, and I turned to leave the kitchen.

"What do you mean the case isn't over yet? John?"

I kept walking. It was another bad decision.

"John? I'm asking you a question. What do you mean the case isn't over yet?"

I wanted to keep going, but the tone and the volume told me I couldn't abandon the argument just yet. I turned around, stumbled over the haphazard collection of Lego blocks Macy had slapped together and dropped on the ground in her rush to help me with the groceries. I stifled a four-letter word or two while gathering myself. I could feel a poisonous expression trying to take command of my face.

"The case isn't over, OK? We go back on January second to finish it."

The curiosity caused her to soften, just a bit. "Well, that's strange. Closing arguments were supposed to be today. The case was supposed to be over. Why didn't you get a verdict?"

"It's a long story."

"Sounds like a long story you don't want to tell. Because length of story never stopped you before, not when it was something you felt like telling me about."

"It's complicated. We can talk about it later."

She smiled at that. Not a happy smile. A smug, knowing smile. A smile that told me she knew that, whatever had happened, it was my fault. I wasn't exactly in a position to dispute it.

"Sure, John. We can talk about it later. There's actually plenty of things we need to talk about later."

"What does that mean?"

She kept smiling. "We can talk about it later. For now, I've got to get ready for tonight."

"I told you I can help."

"I didn't expect any help. Just let me handle it. Go do whatever you need to do. If I change my mind, I'll let you know."

"Why are you making this harder than it needs to be?"

She sighed deeply. Her expression became something I

hadn't seen before, or maybe I'd just never noticed it before. "You like asking me that question," she said. "Maybe just once you should ask yourself that question."

I stood there for a while, waiting for something more. But she'd slipped back into party-prep mode. It was like I wasn't even there. For the first time in eighteen years of marriage, I wondered whether she actually wanted me to be.

10

I PUSHED OPEN the door to our bedroom. The suite on the second floor had become the temporary storage facility for the many things had to be tucked out of sight during the party. All the stuff that otherwise cluttered our day-to-day lives. All the stuff that became part of the permanent landscape of the interior of our home. All the stuff that needed to be removed completely from view whenever company came to the house. As if we had to pretend we didn't actually live there, that it was ready for an open house. Ready to be sold. Ready for a new family to take possession, as long as no one went into our bedroom, or opened any of the closets or drawers.

I tried not to focus on the things Linda had dragged into the room in the hours since I'd left for court. Macy's giant plastic kitchen set. The exercise bike we kept in the TV room because it was close enough to the wireless router so that Linda could compete against cyclists from anywhere in the world, as long as they were close enough to a wireless router, too. I wondered how she got it up the stairs. The boys must have carried it. They were getting to the age where they could do pretty much anything and everything I did. Maybe she really didn't need me anymore.

I decided not to take full inventory of the rest of the stuff before peeling off my courtroom uniform. I put on a T-shirt and shorts. I pulled back the covers on our bed. She'd already given me permission to do it. Even if she didn't mean it, I was too tired and too frustrated and too emotionally and physically drained to pretend it wasn't real. I climbed onto the mattress where two of the three kids had been conceived. I pulled the covers completely over my head. I buried my cheek into the pillow, weird wrinkle growing next to the left side of my nose be damned. I slept. I escaped.

It was temporary, as it always is. The act of falling asleep is the only minute or two of true relaxation. It melts into dreams influenced by that patchwork of fleeting thoughts and random interactions before it all abruptly ends. Whether interrupted by an alarm going off or a prostate screaming for relief or some stray noise, the sleep experience is overrated.

Fall asleep. Wake up. Back to reality.

Reality came back three hours after I fell asleep. I hadn't set an alarm, and none of the periodic ruckuses from downstairs had pierced through the slumber. Not after a full week in trial. Well, most of a week. I checked my phone. It was half past five. People would start showing up in an hour. All I could really do at that point was to get myself ready and stay out of the way.

I slogged through the darkness of the room. I flipped the switch for the lights over the double sink in the master bathroom. The combination of pressure and time had left my scalp badly in need of a reset. I showered, shampooed, dried my hair. I probably should have shaved again, but I didn't want to risk cutting my face.

The light bulbs above my head made the collection of gray hairs more noticeable. Linda had told me to consider using a little dye to hold things in place. I didn't want to play that game, because it always ends only one way—old man with ridiculously dark hair until he admits what everyone else knows, drops the facade, and looks like he aged a quarter of a century overnight. Nope, I had already decided to take the grays as they came, in a slow-moving parade that would allow me to sink gradually into the quicksand of old age and whatever lurked beneath it.

Linda blew into the room like a heat wave, or maybe the opposite. She was talking to herself as she often did, telling herself everything she needed to do and interspersing various grievances and complaints, parsed out with passive-aggressive expertise. She used to do it with the kids, when they were too small to understand what she was saying. Sometimes, she'd do it with the dog or the cat. When all else failed, Linda talked to Linda. Most of the time, her messages were meant for me.

"They're bringing the trays soon," she said to no one. "I need to get myself dressed and make one last pass through the house because God knows whether someone made a mess since the last time I cleaned everything up."

I kept my mouth shut and my head low, working my way to the ever-shrinking portion of the walk-in closet where some of my clothes were haphazardly arranged on hangers of various size, structure, and age. Other items had landed in my one assigned drawer of the dresser. Still others were loosely folded into uneven piles on the floor of the closet, where my shoes should have been but they were strewn with the rest of the family's footwear like the aftermath of a Picway earthquake on the floor of the garage, just to the left of the entrance to the house.

"What should I wear?" I said from inside the closet.

"Why are you asking me?"

"Because if I choose something on my own, you'll say, 'You're wearing that?'"

"And you'll still wear it anyway."

I walked back out to the bedroom. She was moving toward the bathroom, for makeup and whatever else she did in there. Even after all these years, I didn't know the full routine. I just knew to avoid it.

"I'm trying to cooperate," I said. "You tell me what to wear, and I'll wear it."

She shrugged as she moved. "Wear something nice. It's not like we'll be shoulder to shoulder."

"Well," I said, "we are hosting this thing."

She stopped and locked eyes with mine. "No, John. I'm hosting this thing. You're spectating. The minute enough people show up to give you cover, you'll be shooting pool in the basement."

"I'll have at least three of our other guests down there with me," I said, as if I'd accidentally solved a Rubik's cube with my eyes closed. I raised a finger in victory. "Entertaining them."

She rolled her eyes at that. I hated when she rolled her eyes at me. But I didn't say anything, because whenever I got a good eye roll, I almost always deserved it.

"Just wear whatever you want to wear," she said. "I'm late. And I still have plenty of things to do."

I paused. Held my breath. Sounded out in my mind a couple of potential options for what to say next. I picked one. "What can I do to help?"

"They're delivering the food soon. You can be on the lookout for the van. I've already paid them."

"Do I need to tip them?"

"I said I already paid them, John. Do you ever listen to me?"

I disengaged at that point. I found a pair of black jeans, still fairly new and not all that faded. Pulled a maroon sweater from the floor of the closet. It was big enough to conceal the majority of my paunch, at least from most angles. I didn't look in the mirror because I told myself I didn't care. (The truth was I didn't want to be depressed by what I'd see.) Besides, I didn't need any further reminders of what I'd become. Soft, lumpy, wrinkled, graying. With each fresh December pulling me another year closer and closer and closer to whatever I'd ultimately become.

I thought of the old man. Do I really want that? Frail and shrunken and withered? There's something to be said for going to sleep at around seventy and not waking up. I told myself I'd probably feel differently about that in twenty-five years. Maybe eighty. No older than eighty. Eighty and out.

My own parents didn't come close to eighty, or even seventy. Mom had cancer, fought it for five years. Died at fifty-four. Dad had bypass surgery six months later, seemed fine, then dropped dead. He was fifty-seven. They'd both been gone more than twenty years. I'd met Linda eighteen months before my mother had died, and I'd embarked on my own life. It made it easier to move on, but there was never anything easy about it.

Linda still had her parents. She had no idea what it was like, and nothing I told her about it would make her understand. It had to be experienced, the permanent shift in existence that happens when your parents are gone forever. Nothing, not one thing, can prepare you for how it feels when it actually takes place.

Linda's parents had a small house just a few miles from us. The best part about the arrangement was they never, ever spent the night. Not that I didn't love them or respect them. But no parents ever completely and fully surrender a daughter to some guy they didn't hand pick for her. I already knew I'd be the same way with Macy.

I went to find Macy and the boys, to make sure they weren't undoing any of the things Linda had done to get ready for the party. I wasn't angling for credit. I was just hoping to avoid blame. Once I exited the bedroom for the rest of the house, anything that happened anywhere on the premises could and would be used against me.

When I made it down the steps, I soaked in the atmosphere. Linda had outdone herself, as she often did. The place was immaculate, the decorations sparkled. The candles threw flashes of light in a way that made the place seem genuinely cozy and inviting.

It instantly became neither when I vomited onto the floor of the TV room, just off the kitchen. I stood there, stunned by the speed and intensity of it all, especially since I hadn't eaten anything since losing everything I'd previously eaten, earlier that day. No one heard me, which was both a relief and a surprise, since it sounded like a freight train with rusty wheels had roared out of my gullet. I went to find the paper towels, a precious commodity that would hopefully be replenished by my sister-in-law since I'd forgotten to get more of them at the store. Regardless, the only other options were to use actual towels or to leave the mess where it was. I made an executive decision that Linda would appreciate neither of those outcomes.

I hustled to collect the goop I'd deposited, stunned by the fact I even had anything in there to spill onto a wooden floor that needed a good refinishing that I lacked the skill or desire to apply. Only a bit of it had gotten onto the area rug that framed the space between the black leather couch and the sixty-five-inch flatscreen TV, a one-time luxury purchase that now could be had at any U-Sav-Plentee for relative peanuts. I tried my best to get it all and to blot the orangey stain on the tassels of the plush rectangle we had unfurled in that exact spot when we bought the house. I managed this three-ring circus of digestive shame as best I could, thankful the boys weren't in sight (the video games were in the basement) and Linda had yet to descend the stairs.

The doorbell rang. I ran with the last of the paper towels to the trash can in the kitchen, making a mental note to change out the bag after the food had been put in place. I wondered exactly where the trays were supposed to go. Just as the thought crossed my mind, I heard Linda coming down the steps to get the door.

"What's that smell?" she said with a crinkled nose as she breezed past me to the main entrance to the house, a large, thick door painted white on the inside and red on the outside.

"I think it's the candles," I said. "Or something else. I'm not sure."

She gave me a look suggesting both confusion and suspicion before the doorbell rang again, snapping her out of it and forcing her to focus on the delivery of the meal for our party. Her party.

She had the kids from the restaurant take the trays to the island in the kitchen. They followed every command without hesitation. She must have tipped them well. I stood out of the way, marveling at the efficiency of it all. I didn't know much in that moment, but I knew Linda wouldn't have puked in court that morning.

I scanned the floor and other surroundings to make sure I'd gotten it all. I remembered I needed to change out the trash can. I cared less about the mess I'd made and more about facing a stream of questions that possibly would have had me in the emergency room after the last straggler left the house that night. I'd resolved to get checked out following round one. After having it happen again fewer than twelve hours later, getting an appointment with a real doctor would be the first order of business for the morning after Christmas.

If you live that long.

My head jerked as the thought invaded my brain. I wanted to ignore the possibility that it was anything that serious. On a day that already had been anything but calm and bright and peaceful on earth and every other tired old lyric from every Christmas song that ever had been or would be written, I couldn't let myself entertain the possibility of dropping dead before December 26, especially when we were about to entertain a houseful of people I didn't really want in my home. Really, the absolute last thing I wanted to do for the balance of the night was to deal with our guests, who would be arriving soon.

"John," Linda said, "let's go. Our guests will be arriving soon."

11

THE PROCESSION TO the makeshift pool room in the partially-finished basement began without me, after Artie Phillips and Trent Utz asked if I wanted to play (which of course meant they wanted to play). I told them to go ahead, that I'd meet them down there. I half-smiled when I noticed a couple of other guys slinking toward the doorway to the lowest level of the house before slipping from view.

The faint sound of the clacking balls warmed my heart, even if it didn't pull me down there. I just didn't feel like playing. I also didn't feel like not playing. I basically didn't feel like doing anything. I went through the motions, pretending to be the supportive spouse of the hostess as she welcomed her many friends from the grade school where she teaches. When you work alone like me, and when you spend your entire professional time fighting with other lawyers, opportunities for the creation of meaningful relationships don't come along very often. You eventually get to the point where you don't want them to.

Linda would have been pleased, if she'd been paying attention. I was helpful. Talkative. Almost charming. Even if I felt disconnected from all of it, making stupid little chitter-chatter while also delighted that everyone I encountered was sufficiently absorbed in their own lives (as I was in mine) that they didn't know or care that my opportunity to catch the U-Sav-Plentee tiger by the tail had been delayed by a very unforeseen development.

I asked broad, open-ended questions. It didn't require me to access specific memories about past conversations with the same people. I listened (even if I wasn't listening) to boasts and complaints and concerns and whatever else flowed from voices gradually lubricated by the various bottles of screw-top wine and twist-top beer and bargain-basement bourbon that Linda had purchased during a recent trip to the liquor store, while I was preparing for the next day of trial.

I became the unofficial greeter as more and more of Linda's friends and their spouses or whoever they were arrived. A hearty welcome, with a *may-I-take-your-coat?* flourish. They entered cheerfully, and I hoped more than a few of them would mention to Linda that she'd found herself a good man. Even if I knew deep down I wasn't nearly as good as I needed to be, for her or for the kids or really for anyone. Except maybe the cat, because all the cat needed was a can of food once per day, a reasonably clean litter box, and then just get out of the way and let me do my own thing.

I often found myself envying that damn cat.

I heard the doorbell again. I politely and gracefully disengaged from someone named Martha or Marty or maybe Marianne and went to welcome the next mini-wave of would-be holiday revelers.

As I pulled the door open, I heard the hinges creak more loudly than usual, a screeching whine that caused me to pull my head back to see if a piece of metal had perhaps become loose or broken. When I turned back to the entrance, I felt a shudder and a shake.

There he was again. And this time he wasn't alone.

"Are we late?" the old man said from under his fedora and behind those large, smoky lenses.

"I—well, I guess you're right on time."

He nodded and smiled, sparking a flood of wrinkles around his mouth and up his cheeks and beyond. "She said we were late and I told her we weren't. Maybe fashionably late. Isn't that what they call it?"

"I suppose they do," I said, pulling the door wider. The old man took a shaky step with his left leg across the threshold.

"Thank you for the invitation," he said, although I couldn't remember inviting him. Maybe I had. But I definitely hadn't given him the address.

I saw her standing behind him. The one who had stayed in the car the three prior times I'd seen him that day. She was small and thin and even more frail than he was. A malnourished bird without the energy to fly south for the winter.

Her white hair glistened in the light above our stoop. Her face was much smoother than her husband's, not nearly as weathered and worn. She also had glasses, not as large as his but just as thick where it mattered, creating clouds behind which I could catch a faint glimpse of dancing eyes.

"It's you," she said to me. "I told him I wanted to see you. Did he not tell you I wanted to see you?"

The old man turned toward her. "I told you that I told him. Did you think I was lying to you?"

"He can be a little forgetful," she said to me as if he wasn't standing right there, and she extended a hand in less of a greeting and more of an unspoken request for assistance. I thought I felt something when she gripped my palm.

"Welcome to our home," I said to her. It was the only phrase I could muster through the confusion.

"I told him I didn't want to impose, but he insisted."

"It's not an imposition at all," I told her. "Please, come in."

She held onto my hand longer than she needed to, but it didn't bother me. Her grip was cool but also warm, if that makes any sense. It didn't make much sense to me at the time, and I didn't try to figure it out.

I offered to take their coats. They declined. She said they couldn't stay long. He reminded me they were on their way home. I accepted his explanation without asking questions or even having any sprout into my brain. I was both dumbfounded and in a strange way happy they were there.

I led them over to the couch in the TV room. It was empty amid the conversations among the guests and the staccato sounds of cutlery on plates (Linda hated using disposable plastic dishes, no matter how many people were present) and the rest of the noises flowing naturally from the very unnatural presence of so many people throughout the first floor of the house.

"You have a very nice home," the old woman said to me. "Very nice. I'm proud."

"Thank you," I said, accepting what she said without asking myself or her or him why she would say that. I offered to get them some food. I thought they would decline that, too, but the old man said he was starving. That was my cue.

I twisted my way through the crowd with determination, smiling and nodding and saying "excuse me" when necessary in order to get to the kitchen. I fetched a pair of plates and arranged a little of everything on them from the trays of food. I could feel against my face stray wisps of warmth rising from it all. I got them small pieces of lasagna, a tiny mound of pasta with little chunks of chicken scattered throughout (if they wanted seconds, so be it), and a spoonful or two of mixed vegetables. I checked the presentation before collecting two forks and commencing the trek back to the couch.

"Hungry?" Linda said as I began to move away from the island.

I looked down at the plates and then back at her. "It's not for me. It's for a couple of our guests."

"The idea was the guests would get their own food. That's what everyone else is doing."

"I'm just trying to be helpful. They're elderly. I didn't want them to have to work their way through the crowd."

"Elderly?" Her nose crinkled again. "I don't think I invited Mrs. Tolliver. She retired last year."

"It's not her," I said. "It's someone else."

"Who is it then?"

"Well, I mean, I'm not really sure. But they're here. I wanted to take care of them."

She seemed surprised, perhaps more by my willingness to help than by the presence of two people she didn't recall asking to come. "That's fine," she said. "It's less that you and the kids will be eating this weekend."

A conversation between a pair of Linda's colleagues caught her attention and she spun away to join them. I seized the opportunity to make my way back toward my guests, technically. It was a slightly more challenging journey, given that I was holding a plate in each hand with a fork perched gingerly atop each one.

I made it back to the couch without incident. They were sitting there, not talking. Just looking around at the conversations and activity. I handed the first plate to the woman, easing it toward a pair of open palms that hovered over her lap. The old man snatched his from my other hand at the same time.

"This looks good," he said to me. "Did you cook it?"

"We ordered in."

"Ordered in? How fancy. Maybe that's why you don't have a nicer car."

I laughed at him, and before I could respond he was working the fork toward his mouth faster than I'd seen him move all day.

"My goodness," the woman said to him. "You act like you've never eaten before."

"Sorry, but you don't cook food like this," he said to her.

"Well, not anymore." She inspected her plate far more carefully than her husband had.

"Ain't that the truth," he said through a full mouth.

"Dear," she said to me, "do you have a napkin?"

I realized I'd forgotten them. I made my way back to the kitchen, once again moving carefully and respectfully around people who seemed to be having a far better time than me.

"Back for more?" I heard Linda say as I scanned the spread for the basket of napkins. I spotted it, grabbed two, and started back.

"I forgot these," I said to her with a wink that was supposed to be playful, but I'm not quite sure how it came off because, well, I was never very playful. She shook her head and went back to talking about whatever it was she and the others had been so fervently discussing. It occurred to me that, even if none of the people present had said anything to me about what had happened that morning, one or more of them might say something to Linda. I felt something stir in my stomach at the thought of her hearing about it from someone other than me. I prayed I wouldn't throw up again, at least not until everyone was gone.

When I got back, I saw that the old man had eaten most of his food. The woman was waiting for her napkin before starting. I handed one to each of them. She smiled at the gesture. The old man snatched his, regarding it as an interruption more than anything else.

"Would you like some more?" I said to him.

"Not yet. I'll let round one digest a little bit."

"He doesn't need any more," she said. "He needs to leave some for the others."

"There's plenty," I said, but the old man seemed to defer to her. I noticed him watching to see whether she'd start eating. Maybe he planned to finish whatever she didn't.

Eventually, she began to lift small amounts delicately toward her mouth. She seemed to be studying every bite. Or perhaps savoring it.

"It's very good," she said. "But there's always something different about a home-cooked meal."

"There is," I said to her, smiling as I watched her tentative movements. It was almost as if she moved her fork to the food and the fork to her mouth robotically. "Linda will be cooking our meals on Christmas Eve and Christmas Day." I felt a bit defensive while saying it. I didn't want them to think we never made our own food.

Then the old man belched, without making any effort to cover his mouth.

"My goodness," the woman said. "I do apologize for my husband. He's not used to eating in the presence of others."

"It's a compliment to the chef," he said. "Whoever he is."

I smiled and nodded. They delighted me, these strangers who entered my life on this strangest of days. I watched the woman eat, slowly and deliberately with those same mechanical movements. She stopped with plenty of food left on her plate.

"I think I'm full," she said. "I hate to waste the rest."

"It's fine," I told her. "Eat what you can." I thought the old man would volunteer to finish it off, but he didn't. He instead requested a drink of water, mentioning that he'd prefer a belt of something stronger but that he knew he shouldn't. I nodded at him, and I said once again that I'd be back.

I started another path toward the kitchen, retrieving a glass from the assembly Linda had placed near the wine. I felt a little dizzy but pushed through it. I realized I hadn't eaten anything since the morning, but I didn't want to press my luck. Not with so many who would potentially witness what would have been the third expulsion of the contents of my stomach that day.

I focused on getting three cubes of ice into the glass. I found a bottle of the fancy water Linda bought for herself and the kids in the refrigerator. I removed the cap and poured until the glass was nearly full. I started back. I could feel Linda's eyes on me, but I avoided saying anything to her.

When I returned to the couch, they were gone. I jerked my head in all directions, looking for their tiny bodies among the others. I peered through the gaps in the arms and heads and torsos, searching for them.

"Where did they go?" I said.

I went toward the steps and strained my eyes into the darkness of the second floor. I knew that, wherever they were, they couldn't have made the climb so quickly. I turned back around, scanning for any sign of the couple. I waited there for a while, sipping the water and hoping I'd see them.

After a little while, I strode with determined nonchalance to the front door, opened it, stepped outside. There was no sign of them out there, either. I shrugged. I went back inside, carrying the glass of water through the TV room and into the kitchen and to the dining room beyond it, wondering if I'd see them in there but knowing deep down I wouldn't.

One of Linda's friends approached me and asked how things were going with the practice. I told her everything was fine. She told me about a friend of hers who was having trouble at work and she'd tell him to call me next week. I forced myself to focus on the conversation, to feign interest in the situation before saying, yes, the person should call and, sure, I'd figure out whether anything could be done about whatever it was.

I resumed my prior role, running out the clock until the time came to gather coats, two at a time, as our guests began to leave. I wondered whether, as the throng thinned, the old man and his wife possibly would emerge from wherever they'd wandered off to. Even though I knew in my heart I wouldn't see them again that night.

Before long, the last of the stragglers had left, with Linda taking them to the door and conversing about whatever it was that I wasn't paying attention to. Linda seemed lively and happy, with the demeanor of someone deeply pleased with how the evening had gone. I kept sipping on the water until the ice had mostly melted. I sucked on one of the shrunken cubes as Linda said her final farewells.

"Well, that was fun," she said to me.

"It went well."

"You seemed to enjoy it."

"I did. Did you think I wouldn't?"

"You never do."

"Well, tonight I did. A little bit, at least."

"Did you ever figure out who those people were?"

"Who?" I said.

"The ones you got the food for."

"I don't know who they were."

"Did they enjoy themselves?"

"I think they did. They just sort of left, I think."

"What do you mean you think?"

"They were here, and then they weren't."

"Did you offend them or something?"

"Offend them? I was very nice to them. They left."

She began to wander through the first floor. It seemed deserted and hollow, with everyone gone. "Where are the kids?" she said.

"In the basement, I think. I'm sure the boys are playing that video game, whatever it is. Macy's probably watching something on her tablet. And Buster is probably right by her side. You know how he gets when a lot of people are around."

"Help me put the food away," she said. "I'll clean everything else up in the morning."

I watched as she moved to the kitchen. She stopped and turned her head toward the couch. She walked over there, and she pointed at the coffee table in front of it.

"Didn't they eat?"

"What do you mean?" I said, tracking my eyes from her finger to glass surface, where two plates sat. They both had a full collection of food on them.

"Aren't those the dishes I saw you fix?"

I shook my head. "Yes, but they ate. I watched them."

"Well, unless two other people got plates of food and brought them to this table and put them down and didn't eat, that looks exactly like what I saw you carry out of the kitchen."

I stumbled toward the table and peered down at it. Sure enough, that was what I had prepared. With a fork perched on top of each pile of food. And a pair of napkins was sitting there, next to the plates.

"I saw them eat," I said.

"I don't know," she said. "A lot of people were here. Just dump it all into the disposal, I guess."

She went to the kitchen. I stayed there, studying the plates. I recognized my handiwork. I felt woozy. I sat on the couch, still staring at the dishes.

"I saw them eat," I said.

"What's that?" she said from the kitchen.

"Nothing," I said. And then I picked up one of the plates and began to eat the food I had watched them eat.

12

I DEVOURED THE contents of both plates, maybe because I thought if the food was gone it would mean they actually had been there. But they actually had been there. I'd seen them. I'd spoken to them. As far as I knew, no one had reported to Linda that her husband seemed to be talking to himself on the couch.

Sleep came very easily, despite my long, late-afternoon nap. Exhaustion from a week in trial and days spent before that in every-waking-moment preparation had taken a toll. In more ways that one, apparently. I slumbered without dreaming, or at least without remembering any of my dreams. The next day, there wouldn't be much time to reflect on them.

Saturday morning. Two days to Christmas. The house would carry that rare, temporary buzz. The party had helped. Even without it, it was time for things to begin feeling festive and merry. As long as I didn't think about everything that had happened the day before, and as long as I avoided talking about it to Linda. So far, so good.

She rolled out from her side of the bed while I was still asleep. I stayed warm under the covers and was relieved I hadn't gotten sick in the middle of the night. Sometimes it just feels good to be there, still and awake and fully conscious of the feel of the sheets on the bottom and the quilt on top, the one my mother had knitted at least thirty years earlier. Beneath the thing it had taken her weeks to make, it still felt like she was pulling me in for a hug I didn't really want but didn't realize how badly I needed.

I heard yelling from the first floor. Joseph called for me. He claimed I'd promised to take him to basketball practice that morning. I had no reason to doubt I'd said I'd take him, even if I didn't remember doing it. And, as he usually did, he'd ignored the creeping of the minutes toward ten o'clock sharp, when practice was due to begin.

I stumbled from the cocoon, feeling more like caterpillar than butterfly. The toothbrush beckoned, but I knew from the urgency in Joseph's voice that I didn't have time for the luxuries of personal hygiene. When he needed to go, he needed to go. And he didn't bother to say he needed to go until the exact instant he definitely needed to go.

I pulled a pair of jeans that seemed to be getting more snug with each passing weekend over legs that were starting to form a small farm of random white hairs. I found a baggy sweatshirt. Or at least a sweatshirt that used to be baggy. Maybe I'd need to bump up a size, in order to have enough extra material to conceal a spare tire that was becoming more and more inflated.

I began fumbling for my keys and wallet, rifling through the pockets of the black jeans I'd worn the night before and then realizing they were still in the suit pants I'd worn to court. I pulled my phone from the surface of the dresser. I noticed that Sandy Matherson had called. Or maybe it was her husband. I didn't feel like talking to either of them. Maybe I'd return the call after dropping Joseph off at the gym. Maybe I wouldn't.

Joseph kept calling my name, even after I'd made it clear I was coming. I nearly tripped and fell down the steps. He stood there at the bottom, wearing only shorts and a Packers jacket over his sleeveless T-shirt. He carried a bag that held a pair of the same Jordans he was wearing on his feet, laces untied. He'd convinced Linda to buy two sets of the identical shoe. One to wear only when playing, the other to wear when not playing. She didn't include me in the decision-making process, because she knew what I'd say about that.

"You ready or what?" he said with impatience that danced on the line of disrespect, noticing my arrival without looking up from his screen.

"Let's go," I said. "Why'd you wait so long to get me up?"

"We had time."

I flew past him and presumed he was following. "We had time," I said. "Key word. Had. We don't have much time now."

"Why are you so bent out of shape? I'm the one who'll have to run if I'm late."

"Persepio is Italian for we always show up on time."

Joseph shook his head and rolled. "That wasn't even funny the first time you ever said it."

I kept moving, through the TV room and into the kitchen and toward the door to the garage. The dog rushed over to me and jumped up, pressing one paw into my stomach and the other right into my crotch. I let out a loud noise that became muffled a bit as I bent over, bracing for that inevitable rush of pain coming from somewhere in my intestines. The dog acknowledged the tip of my nose by depositing a thick layer of concentrated saliva across it.

"Well, that's one way for him to get your attention," Linda said from the other side of the island. She and Macy were making eggs. Macy laughed at me, in a happy and innocent way.

"Why didn't you get me up earlier?" I said to Linda.

"I figured you set your alarm."

"Well, I didn't."

"Why didn't you?"

"You should have been the lawyer," I said.

"It's a simple question."

"I didn't realize I needed to be up."

"Who's fault is that?" she said it with a smile. I either didn't notice or didn't care.

"Shit, Linda, are we really going to do this now?"

"Sthwear jar!" Macy yelled, and she ran toward the other room to fetch it.

"Honey, I don't have any cash on me," I called out to her. "I'll get it later."

I turned back to Linda. The smile was gone. "Real nice, John."

"What?" I said, before realizing Joseph had slipped past me and climbed into the Subaru. He pressed hard on the horn.

"Damn it!" I yelled.

"Sthwear! Jar! Again!"

"Just go," Linda said. "You find a way ruin every good mood we ever have."

I didn't know what to say to that. Macy still seemed to be in a pretty good mood, especially after picking up an IOU for two free dollars to go with all the rest. I looked at Linda, considered my options, and decided to leave before Joseph shoved his hands onto the face of the steering wheel again.

I half-limped toward the car, still feeling the effects of Buster's greeting. Before I reached the handle, Joseph pressed the button on the visor, sending the door up and a blast of wintry air inside. It struck my face and neck. I hurried to get inside the car.

"It's about time," he said as I fell into the seat, straining the leather that was threatening to tear open after three-plus years of my increasingly oversized butt lumbering into the cockpit.

"The dog got me right in the balls. I had to gather myself."

He smiled as I slipped the Subaru into gear and backed out of the driveway. "The old Buster nut buster."

"Is that what you call it?"

"He does it all the time. You need to turn to the side. You're just figuring that out now?"

"I don't know," I said. I checked the clock on the dashboard. We had five minutes to make a seven-minute drive.

"Can you step on it a little?"

"I should go slow just so you're late. It'll teach you a lesson about waiting until the last minute to let me know you need to go."

"Merry Christmas to you, too, Dad."

I pressed down on the pedal. I'd get him there on time. As much as I wanted to be an ass about it, I couldn't do that to him. "Just get me up a few minutes earlier next time, OK?"

By then, he already had his nose back in his screen. "What's that?"

"Nothing," I said. I focused on getting the car to the school on time. It was nice to have nothing else to think about, even for five minutes.

I pulled up near the two steel doors leading into the gym, stopping long enough for Joseph to get out without saying anything. I had no idea how long practice would last. I'd learned from experience that, with this particular coach, practice lasted as long as it lasted. Sometimes, forty-five minutes. Other times, more than two hours.

I pulled the car between a pair of parallel yellow lines in

the parking lot and waited for Joseph, knowing that if I went home the practice would end quickly and that if I stayed I'd be sitting and waiting longer than I wanted to. But I didn't have anything else I needed to do, and Linda was already pissed at me. Not that I didn't deserve it.

Yes, she got mad at me pretty often. Sometimes, it wasn't my fault. Most of the time, it was. And most of the time that it was, I knew damn well I was about to make her mad, and I did it anyway.

I checked my phone, looking at the list of calls I'd missed during the past couple of days of focusing entirely on the trial. I didn't feel like talking to anyone. I didn't feel like doing anything. I knew the feeling all too well. It was the post-trial rut. After days of adrenaline and caffeine and raw terror from constantly performing on a high wire without a net before those who would decide my client's fate, it was a long fall back to normalcy.

It felt worse this time, because the trial wasn't over. It had all slipped into a week or so of limbo, with the chances of a good outcome far slimmer than they'd been the day before. I replayed the events in my mind. The unexpected escape of my breakfast. Did I know it was coming? Could I have done anything about it? How different things might have been if I'd just performed the closing argument and the jury had delivered a verdict for Sandy.

I could feel my stomach rumbling again at the thought of what had happened, and I started to scan the parking lot for a suitable place to deposit whatever was left in my stomach from the two plates of food the old couple hadn't eaten but I had. There was a row of shrubs along the back of the school, about twenty feet across the asphalt lot from where I'd parked. I could make a beeline for the bush line and let nature take its ugly, smelly course.

I turned back from my effort to formulate a vomit contingency plan. I noticed something off to my left. I shook my head. There he was. Fedora and glasses and the same coat he'd worn every time I'd seen him on Friday. As best I could tell, he was wearing the same clothes under it.

I pressed the button that powered down the window. He watched it glide.

"Fancy shmancy," he said, admiring the speed and silence with which the window zipped into the opening in the door.

"Where'd you come from?"

"Did no one ever explain the birds and the bees to you?"

"I mean—never mind. Where's your car?"

He motioned with his right hand behind the Subaru. I craned my head around and saw the oversized Chevy. It looked like it should have a mizzen mast instead of a steering wheel. I noticed the top of the woman's head in the passenger seat, sitting there still and serene.

"What happened to you last night?" I said.

"She wanted to go. She gave me the rush act. I told her we should wait. But marriage is a democracy only when the vote isn't one to one."

"Where are you heading?"

"We're on our way home." He said it just as earnestly and honestly as he had a day earlier. I laughed out loud, but I was careful not to mock him.

"What's so funny?" he said. "You don't believe me?"

"I believe you. I just think you may be lost."

"I don't think so. I know precisely who I am and where I am and what I am." He paused and dipped his head, peering at me with naked eyes over the top of the frames of his glasses. "Do you?"

His words stunned me. They struck me deeply. Not with pain, but with the vague sense of wonder that comes from opening a gift and moving the tissue paper out of the way and finding something unexpected and special and meaningful inside. I became self-conscious of the sudden tears that were clouding my vision.

"I don't know," I said. "Sometimes, I don't know."

"That would seem to be fairly important information. But what do I know?"

I wiped a thick drop from the edge of an emerging crow's foot with the top of my left hand. "I guess I'm just confused. You keep saying you're on your way home. But you don't seem to be making any progress."

He nodded, in a way that almost seemed deliberately condescending. "I think we are. Some journeys can take a little longer than others."

"But you haven't gone anywhere. Yesterday, you were on your way out of town. You got your tire fixed, and then you didn't leave."

"Are we not welcome here?"

"No. I mean, yes. You are. You just don't seem like you're actually on your way home."

"All I can tell you is that we are."

"Is it just the two of you going home?"

He turned back to the car, raising a weathered and leathery hand to wave to his wife. Then he looked at me again. "That depends," he said.

"Depends? Depends on what?"

"It just depends," he said. "Hey, can you loan me some money?"

I coughed at the request. "Money? Like cash? I don't have any cash."

"Who doesn't have cash?"

"Apparently, you don't."

"I didn't say I don't have cash. I just asked if you would loan me some of yours."

"I'd give you anything I had," I said. "But I don't carry cash." I fished the wallet out of my front pocket and removed the green plastic bank card. "I use this. Everywhere I go. It's easier than cash."

"Well, give me that then."

"You can't use this. Only I can."

"So it's not really cash. Cash is cash. That's like a credit card. I used to have a credit card."

"It's a credit card and it's cash. It comes right out of your bank account. Do you really not have one?"

He produced a wad of bills, licked his thumb, and started rifling through them, making a popping sound as he did an impromptu count. "I have cash. Bills. Paper money. That's all that matters."

"Maybe I should be the one asking you for some money."

"You want some? Apparently, you need it."

"I'm fine," I said, chuckling. "You should be careful with how you flash that around. If the wrong person sees it, they might try to take it."

"Why would they try to take it?"

"You know, steal it. People take money from other people."

"Anyone who'd steal money from a broken down old man like me must need it more than I do."

It got quiet for a few seconds. I became aware of the silence. I blurted out what I was thinking.

"Who are you?" I said.

"Who am I?"

"Yeah. Who are you? That was my question."

A smile sprouted and spread. Wrinkles danced along the bottom of his face. White eyebrows snuck out from behind the top of his frames. "That was my answer," he said, and then he turned and shuffled back to the Chevy.

I sat there, dumbfounded. I realized I hadn't wished him a Merry Christmas. I had a feeling I'd still have more chances to do it.

13

I WAITED FOR Joseph. Feelings of confusion and serenity wrestled within me, one never quite able to pin the other against the mat. I didn't try to sort them out, didn't try to prioritize one over the other. I just existed in those minutes. I wasn't sure how many had elapsed. I pulled up the holiday station on the satellite radio and allowed the music to envelop me.

I thought of Christmases gone by. The years with my parents and Baby Michael. I sifted through the memories of the wonder and the anticipation. The days of believing in a magic that made the month of December distinctly different from the other eleven. The hours of watching and hoping and the comfort and the feelings of safety and security and an idea that, by the time those sensations had fully taken over, they would never end.

I didn't think of my parents as much as I used to. I never thought of my brother. I remember realizing for the first time as a kid that my parents someday would be gone. I never imagined Baby Michael would join them in whatever or wherever or however things went once it all ended here. I was still mad at him for leaving. It was the kind of grudge that never would be resolved, because he wasn't around for us to argue or cuss or fight our way through it. The only way I could express my frustration was to ignore his memory.

It had happened so fast. Somewhere beneath my own selfish sense of loss I felt something. Was it guilt? Regret? I didn't know. He'd never shared with me the feelings and the fears and the sickness and whatever else it was that had caused him to do to himself what he did. I remained grateful my parents didn't have to endure the despair I'd experienced when we buried their youngest child.

I didn't want to go to his funeral. I was too angry with him for doing it. But I had no choice. I was the only one left. With my parents gone, it fell to me. All of it. The arrangements, the conversations with the employees of the funeral home who had developed an annoyingly polished routine for dealing with those who were dealing with unimaginable loss. They acted like they knew, but they really had no idea.

The selection of the plot, right across from my parents. I hadn't visited the place since the day they lowered his coffin into the ground. I had no desire to return. I wished I'd picked a different cemetery for him. I didn't know that the torment of seeing his headstone would keep me from ever seeing theirs again. From standing there, reflecting and contemplating and praying or whatever I would do while standing over the spot where they'd forever rest. I considered making the trip that very day, a hundred miles from where I continued to go on while the three of them permanently did not.

I tried to remember where I'd put the old photo album. The one I couldn't bring myself to open and peruse. The one that would supplement so many memories of the three of them. I resolved to find it as soon as I got home. Just as quickly, I decided not to do it—and definitely not to go to their graves—not with Christmas so close.

I needed to be present for my own family. Nothing good would come from wallowing in days gone by, bygone days that would never return. I needed to make memories my own children would be able to access years from now. I wanted them to remember me in a way that filled them not with mixed messages but with a consistent atmosphere of warmth and love and safety and everything else I tried so hard to give them.

Was I doing that? I considered the question carefully. I worked too hard, just like my own father had done. I wanted to set an example that would carry them deep into their own lives. I hoped I was crafting the right one. I doubted whether I actually was.

My mind returned to the past two days, the strange series of events that had been complicated by the old man and woman who had entered my life without warning and who kept showing up, to the point where I was now expecting it. Where would I see them next? I didn't know, but I knew I would.

The songs played, one after another. The songs that bridged a stream of holiday seasons spanning forty long years. It was one hell of a time to have a midlife crisis. I always thought I'd just buy a fast car before settling into that slow march toward the end.

I hated these emotions, but I also embraced them. I had a feeling the next few days would go a long way toward shaping whatever would come next for me. This unexpected, baffling development that I struggled in futility to comprehend. What path had I suddenly found myself on? I didn't know, and I didn't think I'd have much say in where it would take me from here.

I saw some of Joseph's friends beginning to filter out of the gym and migrate to the various other cars that had arrived to take them home. I realized I'd been crying again. I tried to pull myself together.

Joseph emerged from the doors to the gym, face hypnotized by his screen, buds dangling from his ears. He glanced my way long enough to see where I'd parked. I hurried to rub away the lingering tears and turned off the radio. As he opened the door, I felt the cold air rush inside the car.

He sat across from me. He didn't seem to notice anything was wrong before I started the car and drove.

He said nothing. I said nothing. I tried to push aside everything I'd been feeling and thinking, to bring myself back to the present. Back to this Christmas, and to this Christmas only.

The trip home continued in silence. I focused on the road. I eventually could feel him looking at me, as his attention somehow broke from whatever it was he and the rest of his generation did with their phones. I pretended not to notice.

"Dad," he said, "is everything OK?"

"It's fine," I said, forcing a smile. "Everything is fine. It's great. It's Christmas."

"Well, not for two more days."

"You're right," I said, hoping my voice wouldn't crack and my face wouldn't quiver. "Two more days."

"Did you get something for Mom?"

Shit, I hadn't. I hadn't even thought of it. I struggled every year to come up with something that would be sufficient, that would be memorable, that would reflect my appreciation for everything she did. And there was still a little time for me to avoid the annual rush to get something at the last minute; usually with minimal thought or effort.

The fresh notion of this forgotten obligation gave me something that hopefully would let me turn the page on the past couple of days, a project that would require effort and creativity and an amount of cash that wouldn't blow the household budget to smithereens. That was the basic reality of buying gifts for a spouse. The money came from one pot, the same shared dollars that otherwise ensured all bills would be paid on a timely basis.

I embraced the previously neglected challenge of coming up with the right gift for Linda, since it would carry me through the rest of that day and maybe some of the next one, dragging me away from these twists and turns that had me digging up memories that were better left unremembered.

"I'll take care of it," I said to him. "It'll be from all of us."

"Make sure it's something nice."

I told him I would, that she'd be happy with it. I hoped I would be able to accomplish that. Even if, deep down, I doubted I actually could.

14

JOSEPH'S FACE STAYED in his phone until we got home. I noodled through various ideas as to what we could get for Linda while I steered and braked and accelerated and braked and steered the Subaru. It's one thing for her to understand I'd been too busy to shop. It's quite another for the kids to have nothing for their mother. I was the only one who would be able to fix that problem.

I hated this feeling. In all our time together, I rarely knew what to get her. Even when we were dating. I still recall stumbling through the mall, sweaty and anxious, searching for the right gift for her birthday just weeks after we'd started doing whatever we were doing that became something more than that. It couldn't be too nice. It couldn't be too simple. It couldn't be too presumptuous. It couldn't be too unfamiliar. I couldn't remember what I'd ultimately gotten her that day. I couldn't forget the feeling of searching in vain, of eventually settling for anything if only to end the experience of looking.

Now, all these years later, those same old sensations began to creep in again. I racked my brain for anything she might have mentioned. Either she hadn't said anything or I hadn't been listening. Or both. Probably both.

We'd drifted over the years, the wants and necessities of three kids creating a void, or filling one that already existed. We took no time to work on us. I took no interest in it. I didn't know much about who she had become. She didn't know much about me. And now I had to figure something out quickly, on top of everything else that was going on.

I thought of the old man. Part of me wanted to ask him for advice. It was a strange feeling. I pushed it down while I pulled myself out of the Subaru. Maybe I'd find a way to finagle some guidance from Linda as to something sufficient that I could buy between early Saturday afternoon and Sunday night.

Linda and Macy had gone back to baking cookies. The dog hung around, waiting for anything that accidentally or otherwise would have made its way to the ground. I'd tried for months to get the kids not to give Buster anything other than his own food. I would have had better luck getting Buster not to give the kids anything other than their own food.

He didn't bark or yelp or do anything other than sit there, staring in silence while hoping for the opportunity to snatch something he believed would be the most delicious morsel he'd ever encountered. He was determined and focused and diligent in his quest for a piece of pizza crust or a chunk of chicken. I admired the dog's resolve. Except when he resolved to throw a paw into my crotch.

"Hi Daddy!" Macy said, youthful interest in her father still in authentic abundance. "We made more cookies. Lotsth and lotsth of cookies. Do you want one?"

"In a little bit," I said. She made me smile. She always made me smile. I usually always needed it.

"Macy, do you remember Daddy's favorite?" Linda said to her.

"Sthnickerdoodle!" she shouted, stiffening her body to make herself heard by anyone who was inclined to hear what she had to say, and anyone who wasn't.

I scanned the trays and inspected the cookies. The aroma from the various options blended together into that beautiful, comprehensive odor of a bakery, with all the great smells coming together in a cluster of flour and sugar and eggs and chocolate and frosting. I inhaled deeply through my nose and exhaled slowly through my mouth. It was calming.

"Are you counting to ten, Daddy?"

"No, honey," I said, smiling at her while also regretting I'd ever told her about that stupid anger-management device I'd learned from my own father. "It just smells really good in here."

"Maybe it does now, but Busthter has been farting," Macy said.

"Macy!" Linda said to her as she worked on the next batch of dough.

"That'sth not a sthwear jar. Daddy, fart isn't a sthwear jar, is it? That'sth not the real 'F' word, is it?"

My eyes narrowed. "What do you know about the real 'F' word?"

She rolled her eyes at me from behind her glasses, exaggerating the movement. "Everybody knows about the real 'F' word, Daddy."

Linda didn't stop what she was doing. "Macy, do you say the real 'F' word?"

"Never," she said. "That'sth a definite sthwear jar." She turned to me. "Daddy, I never sthaid the real 'F' word. Trustht me."

"I believe you," I said as I kept watching Linda, her thin fingers, delicate but strong, working on the dough and preparing to put another batch in the oven. She didn't notice my eyes on her like she would have years ago, when it was just the two of us. Buster saw an opening to snatch a cookie from the edge of the island and Macy ran after him, as if she was going to retrieve it and return it to the spot it previously held at the corner of the rack.

"Do you need me to do anything today?" I said to Linda.

"I've done everything," she said, again without looking up. We'd argued in the past about her tendency to insist on doing everything and to reserve the right to complain that she had to do everything. I didn't want to revisit that subject, at least not now.

"I've been busy the past few weeks."

She finally shot me a glance, before shrugging her shoulders a bit. "You're always busy."

"But I've been more busy than usual. I've had a trial."

"Trial, no trial. Whatever. You're always busy. And that's fine."

"I don't want anything," I said. "I hope you didn't get me anything."

She looked up at me. She said nothing.

"I mean it," I said.

"Right."

"I have plenty of ties."

She shook her head. "You don't get ties. And you know it. Seriously, John, I know why you're saying this. I don't need anything."

"What are you talking about?"

"That's why you said it. You don't want anything so you won't feel bad about not getting me anything."

I tried to act indignant. It wasn't convincing. I can't even remember what I said. It probably was just a stream of grunts. They subsided. I knew what I was going to say next, that any effort to keep the words inside would have been pointless.

"Is there anything you want?" I said.

"It's way too late to start shopping, John. Way too late."

My indignation became a bit more convincing. "No, it's not. There's still time."

"Where are you going? The mall? The grocery store? How about U-Sav-Plentee?"

"That's a good one."

"There's definitely nothing I'd want that you'd be able to get tonight or tomorrow," she said. "And I don't want a bunch of candy. I don't need it." She glanced at my midsection, hidden poorly inside the sweatshirt I'd found after I rolled out of bed. "You don't need it, either."

"Now we're fat shaming?"

"You're not fat," she said. "Not yet. But you're getting there. My bigger concern is your health. It wouldn't be very good if you dropped dead."

I didn't say anything for a while. She worked on putting thick white globs of goo on the racks while I stood there. "Do you really mean that?" I said.

"Mean what, John?"

"It wouldn't be good if I dropped dead."

She slammed her palms onto the island. Two clouds of flour went airborne. "You got me, John. You figured me out. I hope you drop dead. I want your insurance money. In fact, if you don't drop dead, maybe I'll hire someone to make you drop dead."

"OK," I said. "I get the point."

"Why would that thought even enter your mind, much less come out of your mouth?"

"I don't know." I was embarrassed I'd said it. Until she continued.

"The kids need you."

"The kids? How about you?"

"How about me, John? That's a great question, how about me?"

"I'm confused."

"You don't appreciate me. You don't care about me."

"That's a crock," I said.

"You just expect me to hold everything together while you chase that giant verdict that will make you a star lawyer. The guy who everyone will want to represent them."

"What's wrong with that?"

She stopped. She gathered herself. She found a towel and wiped the small bits of dough from her hands. I turned to look for Macy, hoping she'd come back to the kitchen and short circuit whatever was coming next.

"You're not that lawyer," she said. "You never will be. If you were, it would have happened by now."

"I can't believe you'd say that. Why would you say that?"

"Because it's true. You're forty-five. You've been practicing for almost twenty years. If it was going to happen, it would have happened by now."

"I do well with the work I have."

"Then you need better work. But you don't want to advertise on TV."

"Those guys are bozos."

"Those guys are rich bozos. Their families are secure. For a couple of generations, probably."

"All it takes is one good case, Linda."

"All it takes is one good injury case. Tractor-trailer wipes out a family. Awful as that is, that's how you make huge money. You're representing people who deserved to be fired anyway."

"You don't mean that."

"What company worth a crap fires its good employees?"

"Seriously?" I said. "Plenty of them do. Management gets threatened by troublemakers. They target people who are too expensive, especially if they get injured at work. I vet these cases. I turn plenty of them away."

"Maybe you should turn more of them away."

"What do you mean by that?"

"I mean I don't mind if you work hard, as long as it's leading toward something. You're chopping on a tree you're never going to cut down."

"You don't know that."

"Then why haven't you cut it down, John? Twenty years in, why is the tree still standing?"

"I haven't been doing it from this side for twenty years."

"No, but the time you spent on the other side supposedly gave you the game plan. The treasure map. That's what you called it, remember? *The treasure map.* When you talked me into letting you give up your partnership and roll the dice on going it alone. You knew how to get to that treasure."

"I still do."

"Then where is it, John? Where's the treasure? Again, I don't care if you work as hard as you do. But if you're spinning your wheels in the mud, what are you really working for?"

I realize spouses serve as the ultimate check against delusion or hubris or whatever. I know she meant well. It still hurt me. I tried to act like it didn't, but it did. I turned and began to trudge out of the room, beaten and perhaps even broken by the blast of candor I'd received as an unwanted early Christmas gift. Ho, ho, ho.

As I exited, Macy re-entered, chattering about something she'd seen outside, a rabbit or a squirrel or something. Linda's voice continued. "You know what I'd like?" she said.

I didn't hear her at first, wallowing in my emasculation. I kept walking.

"John," she said in a normal tone of voice.

"Earth to Daddy!" Macy said, helping her mother catch my ear. I turned back to them.

"I'd like a tree," Linda said.

Standing in the family room, I gestured with my chin to the seven-foot, plastic-needled cone we kept in the attic from January 2 until the day after Thanksgiving. "We have a tree."

"I mean a tree. A real tree."

I could feel my eyebrows raising, even as my heart kept slowly receding deeper into my chest. "Where would we put it?"

"Right there. We can move that one into the dining room. Santa can put the presents under the real one."

"We'd need more lights and ornaments," I said.

"You just told me you're willing to go shopping. At least you'd know what to buy."

I stood there, ruminating over the fact that she'd called my bluff. Not that it was a bluff. I'd been willing to do it. But that was before she'd castrated me and then dangled her handiwork in my face.

"Fine," I eventually said. "You want a tree, you got a tree." I turned and continued to slink away.

"You know what else I want?" she said, and she didn't wait for me to ask. "Take the kids with you."

"Yesth! Yesth! Yesth!" Macy said. "We're going to go get a real tree!"

I wondered whether the boys would share even a fraction of her enthusiasm. They probably wouldn't want to go. I realized that, while they'd roll their eyes and say "do we have to?", they wouldn't resist if Linda told them they'd be accompanying Macy and me to purchase and retrieve a real tree.

I pondered this development. It would be a nice distraction from feeling sorry for myself. It would nudge everything back to square one. I hadn't known what to get Linda, and now she told me what she wanted. Between the tree and the lights and the ornaments, it would take some real effort. I had a chance to prove myself to her with this new assignment, even if I apparently hadn't been proving myself with my efforts to provide maximum financial support for the family. I decided I'd worry about that later. For now, I had my marching orders. Tree. Lights. Ornaments. Go.

First step, tree. A real tree. I had no idea where I'd find a real tree. I knew they had them somewhere. I didn't want to ask Linda that question, because I'd probably driven by more than a few places that were selling them as I went back and forth to the courthouse or my office over the past few weeks.

So that was that. It would be simple. I'd get the kids in the car, and we'd go find a tree. Wherever that tree might be.

15

WITH EACH STAIR I climbed, I thought less about Linda's frank assessment of my career trajectory and more about a very specific list of tasks that would help me through the rest of the afternoon and evening.

First step, get a tree.

I took a hot shower and prepared to carve away the collection of stubble that had been sprouting into something more than that in the thirty or so hours since I'd last shaved. I did a double take when I noticed that most of the short hairs were white. Even at forty-five, there were still empty spots next to and below the corners of my mouth, a genetic defect that kept me from ever growing a full beard. Now, even if those areas would decide to begin producing real hairs, the end result would be far less manly than elderly.

Santa Claus did indeed exist; if I went long enough without shaving, I'd become him. Especially with the extra layer of flesh gathering under my jaw. I told myself that, after the holidays, I'd get it under control. If losing my jowls were only as easy as shaving my face.

I remembered that something had caused me to spontaneously puke twice the day before. Maybe whatever was wrong with me would accelerate my plan. Having cancer or some other serious disease would be one hell of a way to lose the weight.

I dried my hair with a towel and combed it into place after sending tiny little pieces of North Pole down the drain. I brushed my teeth. I also flossed, even though my next trip to the dentist was at least three months away. I'd always been good at throwing myself zealously into the task at hand. Today, I'd find the right tree. I'd get the rest of the right things to put on that tree. I'd do it. I'd welcome the distraction from everything else that had knocked me for a loop since I'd left for court the prior morning.

I started calling for the kids as I made my way back down the steps. Macy stood ready by the door to the garage, boots and coat and hat and smile brighter than anything I'd ever find for our eventual new tree. The boys, to no surprise, were nowhere to be seen. I yelled their names in a way I rarely did, barking out the syllables sternly and decisively but without any hint of anger or frustration. The parade of racing feet soon stormed up the stairs from the basement, a herd of domesticated wildebeest suddenly on the move.

I expected Macy and I would have to wait for them to get ready, but they had their clothes and coats on. Mark wore long, baggy shorts, no matter the temperature. I'd given up trying to get him to do otherwise, and I didn't care if other parents judged me for letting him leave the house in late December with bare lower legs.

"Wow," I said to them. "I'm actually impressed by this."

"Mom told us to get ready," Mark said. It didn't surprise me.

Mom was the one who did the parenting, so Mom was the parent to whom they'd respond.

Macy giggled with glee. She ripped the door open and bolted for the car.

"I've got shotgun," Joseph said, in a reminder not a reservation.

"I can't sthit in the front stheat yet anyway," Macy said. "Right, Daddy?"

Mark already had his nose back in his phone as he made the way around the car to the seat behind Joseph. All three of them were in my field of vision. They were growing and changing and I could feel the years preparing to accelerate toward college and weddings and babies of their own and through it all I'd get grayer and fatter and shorter and older.

If only there were a way to have grandchildren without becoming a grandparent.

I opened the door to the Subaru and sat. Instantly, my nose alerted me to a problem. I turned to Joseph.

"Did you shower after practice?"

"Mom said we were going somewhere. I didn't have time."

"Do you smell that?" I said to the kids in the backseat.

"He alwaysth sthmells that way," Macy said, with that same cheer in her voice, maybe even a little more of it because she seemed to think she was putting my mind at ease.

Mark had nothing to say in response, thanks to a phone that was capturing his full attention. Plus, given the amount of time he spent with his brother, Mark's nose likely had become desensitized to the fifteen-year-old's natural funk.

"Where are we going?" Joseph said.

"Mom didn't tell you?" I said.

Just as the words came out, Macy interjected. "We're getting a tree for the housthe! A real, live Christhtmasth tree!"

"Really?" Joseph said.

"Mom wants a real tree."

"What are we doing with the one we have?" Joseph said.

"We'll move it to the dining room. You can help me."

He sat there for a second. I could sense the gears churning from the corner of my eye. "How are we getting it back home?" he said.

I hadn't really thought about that. I accessed whatever knowledge I had about Christmas trees. It wasn't much.

"We'll tie it to the roof."

"How will we tie it to the roof?" Joseph said.

The little bastard was already a budding lawyer.

"We just will," I said. "Where we buy it. They'll know how to do it."

"Can I ride on top with it?" Macy said.

"I don't think Mommy would like that, honey."

"I never get to do anything."

Joseph typically had maybe two words to say on any given topic. For some reason, he had more questions for me on this one than an overly-suspicious customs agent. "Where are we getting the tree?"

"Good question. I think there are places out there."

"Places?"

"I was never shopping for a tree, so I didn't keep track. But I'm pretty sure I've seen places with trees."

"There's one on the way to my sthchool," Macy said.

"See," I said to Joseph. "They're everywhere."

I followed the path to my office, optimistic we'd find a place that sold trees. If that didn't work, we'd head toward Macy's kindergarten. Regardless, a real tree we would find.

"We're not gonna find a tree," Mark said, breaking his phone's trance for an instant.

"Why so negative?" I said.

"I don't know. I just have a feeling we're not gonna find one."

"We'll find one," I said. "I guarantee you we won't go home until we find what we're looking for."

I drove, keeping my eyes open for any evidence of a collection of Christmas trees ready for quick and easy purchase with the insertion of a debit card into whatever makeshift electronic contraption was currently being used to harvest funds at these temporary pop-up spots. Two days until Christmas, surely someone was still selling trees.

I thought of how busy I'd been the prior week, how focused I'd been on Sandy Matherson's trial. Maybe the places I'd noticed had closed. Really, who buys a Christmas tree two days before Christmas? Procrastinators and tightwads, I thought.

And guys desperate to buy a gift for their wives, who blurted out the idea without realizing all the trees are gone. Or maybe she already knew that.

I got closer to my office, one of those large, drafty houses on the main drag near the heart of town that had gradually swapped out families for light commerce—doctors, dentists, lawyers, funeral homes. The full gamut of services the human animal requires, cradle to grave. Literally.

I started to feel that same heat on my neck from all those years ago, when a trip to the mall had failed to yield an acceptable birthday gift for a young woman who probably would have been better off not saying "I do" but "are you nuts?"

"I told you we're not gonna find a tree," Mark said.

"Butt out of this," Joseph snapped at him. I officially didn't have a favorite kid. If I did, Joseph would have vaulted to second place in that moment.

"We'll find a tree," I said. "It just may take some effort."

"I sthaid there's one on the way to my sthcool."

"Where is it, Macy?"

She rolled her eyes. "On the way to my sthcool."

That was all the guidance I'd get. I started back toward

home. Then, I'd follow the path to Macy's school, which was a mile or two away from our front door.

I racked my brain thinking of a place where trees would be sold on that route. But I hadn't taken her to school in weeks. Maybe there was.

I started to ask her for more specifics. I knew I'd get the same answer for a third straight time, so I just kept driving.

We passed our subdivision and rolled toward Macy's school. "Tell me when you see it," I said to her.

"We're not gonna find a tree," Mark said.

Joseph swung his left fist around and thumped his brother in the shin. It wasn't malicious or hateful, just boys being boys. Boys who don't hesitate to resort to non-verbal communication whenever their efforts to reason via vocal cords had failed.

"Hey!" Mark said.

"I told you to butt out. Just keep on checking Kelly Prater's Insta page."

"I'm not."

"Sure you're not."

"Who's Kelly Prater?" I said.

"Mark loves Kelly Prater," Macy said, sing-songing the words.

"Stop it, Macy," Mark said.

I didn't press the issue, not because I wasn't curious about Mark's potentially budding love life but because I spotted up ahead the place we were looking for. There it was, on the right. I saw the trees, lined up in the parking lot next to the veterinary clinic we fortunately didn't have to visit as often as I'd thought we would, after we welcomed Buster and the cat into our home.

"There it is," Macy said, satisfied with herself. "I told you. On the way to my sthchool."

I pulled the Subaru in front of the building and parked.

One other car was there. I could tell it belonged to who-ever was working the lot that day. I felt bad stereotyping the guy (cracked spoiler over a trunk covered in primer gave away the gender), but one thing I knew was people. I knew from the sight of the car that it belonged to a man who abso-lutely would find himself selling Christmas trees two days before Christmas, before doing God-knows-what for cash as of December 26.

Macy swung her door open. She'd become overcome with excitement at the kind of shopping excursion she'd never before experienced. I told her to wait for me before she ran from the car to the selection of oversized plants that previously had been growing peacefully and independently until some-one put a chainsaw through their trunks. The boys seemed to be intrigued by the sight of the trees, even though they tried to stifle any sign that perhaps they were on the verge of pos-sibly enjoying themselves.

A shelter with four narrow metal poles was nestled in the front corner of the lot. The white covering contained a faded Boston Celtics logo. A card table was tucked under the porta-ble cloth roof. Sitting there staring at his phone was the man who undoubtedly owned the car with the cracked spoiler cov-ered in primer.

He looked exactly like I thought he would. I once again felt a pang of guilt, but my hunch had been accurate. Bony frame under a coat that looked to be at least ten years too old and two sizes too big. Ratty mustache over an even rattier beard (unlike me, his inability to grow a full beard hadn't stopped him from trying), and multiple piercings in each ear. He also had something just above his right eyebrow that looked like a lightning bolt. I felt the urge to ask him how he managed to make it stay there.

"Looking for a tree?" he said lazily, without glancing up

from the screen. If it wasn't two days until Christmas, I would have been tempted to make a sarcastic remark in response to his stupid-ass question.

"Yes," I said in a clear voice. I tried to sound like a lawyer. I wanted this guy to see and hear how a professional operates. I wanted to inspire him to become something more than Guy Who Sells Christmas Trees in December, plus whatever else he sells the rest of the year.

I felt guilty again for thinking that. I reminded myself that someone needed to sell Christmas trees, that the broader economy had all sorts and sizes and shapes of jobs and none were any more or less important than the others. That was something my father had told me years before.

I made a mental note to share this with the boys later. I wouldn't be passing judgment, just stating facts. Of course, I also didn't want the boys to aspire to become Guy Who Sells Christmas Trees in December, plus whatever else they'd sell the rest of the year.

"Mister," he said again, this time looking up from his phone. "I asked you what kind of tree you want."

"Earth to Daddy," Macy said.

"What kind of trees do you have?" I said, not really knowing how to respond.

"He has Christhtmasth trees, Daddy."

"Six foot, seven foot, eight foot. Skinny. Full. Straight cut and bulb," he said.

"Bulb?" I said.

"Yeah," he said, "bulb. You know, the kind of tree you plant when you're done."

"Let'sth get the kind we plant!" Macy squealed. "Then we'll have a Christhtmasth tree all year!"

I hadn't considered that possibility. I didn't even know it was one. I looked to the boys for their thoughts, but they were both in their phones. I figured it couldn't hurt to buy a tree that wouldn't end up laying in front of the house, brown and withered and dead in a week or two.

"We'll check them out," I said. "I'll let you know."

"Take your time. Ain't going nowhere. Least not for a couple hours."

Macy took that as her cue to race toward the rows of trees. There were more than I'd realized, maybe at least twenty of them. I wondered how many he'd have left by the next day, and I was curious as to how many he'd sold. I forgot all of that as Macy began to get farther away from me.

"Slow down," I called to her. I turned to the boys. "Will one of you catch up with her, please?"

Joseph gave me a look. I tried to read it. There was vague recognition that, physically, the boys were close to surpassing my own abilities. They didn't know I already knew they had.

I had somehow gotten Mark's attention. He crammed his phone into the right pocket of his baggy shorts and broke into a brisk jog after his sister. Joseph stayed with me. He walked slowly, patiently keeping pace with his old man. I smiled at his decision to not leave me in his dust.

I had a vision of some Christmas to come, where I'd be struggling mightily to keep up with him. He'd wait for me, no matter how long it took. I felt the urge to throw up again.

It passed, thankfully. But it was strong enough to remind me that something wasn't quite right. Still, as much as I never wanted to become the doddering invalid who slowed everyone down, I knew it was still better than the alternative.

I took another step or two before a sound from behind us caught my attention. A deep rumbling of an oversized engine. A muted squealing of worn-out brakes.

I instantly knew what I would see rolling our way, even before I began to turn my head in that direction.

16

THERE IT WAS. The Chevy, carrying two tiny people in the broad front seat. They looked to be even smaller than Macy.

The car churned toward a spot next to the Subaru, so close that if the woman had tried to get out she would have carved a deep dent into the panel on the driver's side of my car. As usual, however, she didn't move. The other door opened instead, a loud creak tearing through the cool and still afternoon air.

I could feel Joseph eyeing me as I watched the old man climb out of the Chevy. I could hear faint cries of Macy shouting, "Thisth one! No thisth one! No, I want thisth one!" as the fedora emerged gradually, a turtle's head starting to peek out of its shell.

"Dad?" Joseph said.

"Hang on a second."

"Aren't we going to look for a tree?"

"Just wait a second."

"What are we waiting for?"

"Don't you see them?"

"See who?"

I turned to face him. "The car that just pulled in. The man who just got out."

Joseph turned toward the place where I'd been looking. "What car?"

"You don't see it?"

"See what?" he said.

That's when it happened again. Another release of the contents of my stomach, right there on the asphalt in the parking lot of the full-time veterinary clinic and part-time Christmas tree emporium. It was orange and yellow and it was chunky and wet and if I'd looked closely enough I might have noticed tiny little streaks of blood in the concoction that instantly spawned a noxious cloud of steam.

The guy sitting at the table sprang to his feet. "Hey, man! What the hell?"

"Sorry," I said, back of my right hand pressed against my lower lip. I wiped away most of what hadn't landed on the ground in front of me.

"You're cleaning that up," he said, gesturing at a puddle that hadn't been there thirty seconds earlier. "I sure as shit ain't doing it."

Macy and Mark had raced back over to me. Macy seemed to be genuinely concerned. Mark was too busy making faces and sounds at the sight and the smell.

I turned toward Mark and scowled. "I dealt with way worse than this from you, once upon a time. Out of both ends."

"Are you OK, Daddy?" Macy said.

"I think so. I must have eaten something that didn't agree with me."

Joseph leaned toward my ear and spoke just above a whisper. "Are we cleaning that up?"

I noticed the steed grid of a storm drain not far from the spot where the mess had landed, maybe five feet away. Joseph followed my eyes. I turned my attention to the building that housed the veterinary practice. "There's a spigot on the wall up there, on the side," I said.

I twisted my face toward the guy who'd made it clear we were on our own. "Do you have a bucket?" I asked.

"Are you gonna puke in that next?"

"No. I'm going to fill it with water, and I'm going to wash this into that drain over there. If that's OK with you."

"Long as it's gone, I don't care how you make it happen," he said.

The man race-walked up toward the trees and emerged before too long with a metal pail that he handed to me carefully, as if more vomit would spray all over him if he happened to get too close to me. "I use this to pour water over the bulbs," he said.

I handed it to Joseph. I took a closer look at the man whose life had brought him to the point where he was selling trees two days before Christmas, while also fetching a bucket for a man who had vomited all over the parking lot where the trees were sold. I tried to look past the sunken cheekbones and the piercings, the hint of a tip of a tattoo sneaking out from the top of the neck of his T-shirt.

I focused only on his eyes. "Do I know you?" I said.

"I suppose you do now."

"No, I mean—never mind. Thanks for the bucket."

"Are you still getting a tree?"

"Daddy, we're still getting a tree, right?" Macy said.

Joseph had already begun guiding the mess toward the drain with water from the pail. He emptied it once and headed back for a refill. "Go ahead," Joseph said. "I'll finish this."

I nodded. I tried to smile. I followed Macy toward the trees.

She began again, insisting on "thisth one" and "thisth one" and "thisth one." The boys eventually caught up with us as we continued to browse. I told them I liked the idea of getting a tree with the bulb on it, although the burlap around the roots and the dirt and everything else below the trunk presented a potential challenge. How would we get this tree to point in the proper direction once it was parked in our TV room, and how would we make it stay that way?

I led the kids back to the tent. The man sat at the table. He seemed nervous. Like I was about to puke on him, without warning. I guess I couldn't blame him.

"Are there special stands for the trees with the bulbs on them?" I asked.

"Can't use a normal stand with those."

"Yes, I know." I tried so hard to be patient. "That's why I'm asking. I need to know how to make that thing stand up in my house."

"You need to get a steel tub. And then you just stick it in there. Press it down until it stands."

"I have a feeling you're making that sound a lot easier than it is."

"You just stick it in the steel tub and push down hard on it," he said. "Eventually, it settles in."

"It doesn't fall over?"

"If you don't push it down hard enough, it could."

"Thanks," I said, still forcing myself not to be rude or sarcastic. "You've been incredibly helpful. I'd like an eight-footer with the bulb on it."

He quoted a price. It was high. I considered giving the kids a lesson in haggling, but at that point I just wanted to get the thing home and then go find a steel tub and lights and ornaments and whatever else we'd trim it with. I asked the guy for some rope to tie it to the car. He started to quote me a price for that until I shot him a look. He charged me only for the tree.

I wasn't quite sure what I was doing. I told the boys we'd put it on the roof of the car, roll down the windows a bit, and run some rope over the tree and then through the openings in the front and back seat. We'd tie a couple of solid knots, and we'd drive home slowly. Fortunately, we didn't have far to go.

Joseph and Mark helped. Joseph took the lead, and Mark did whatever he was told. His phone somehow remained out of his field of vision for more than ten minutes. Macy watched quietly, beaming at the tree and the sight of her father and her brothers getting it ready to become part of the family. At one point, she started singing *O Christmas Tree*, her lisp becoming accentuated the more loudly she projected the tune, or something close to it. I smiled at the sound. Joseph and Mark did, too.

That's when it hit me. We were creating a moment that would provide them with memories of me, decades later. When they gather with their own families on Christmas, when they sit around the table after the meal has been eaten and the plates have been cleared, they'll reminisce about the year Mom wanted a real tree. The year Dad threw up all over the parking lot. The year the boys tied a live tree with the bulb still on it to the top of the car. The year Macy serenaded all of us, poorly.

I felt happy. Truly happy. I tried to remember the last time I'd felt that way. Had it happened since Macy was born? I didn't know.

Once the tree was secure, it was time to get inside the car. It would be a delicate process to open the doors, given how tightly we'd tied it to the roof of the car. I told them to get in one at a time. We dragged the tops of the doors over the ropes with great care. The kids slipped inside, just as soon as they had enough room to fit.

Joseph went first, then Mark. I helped Macy. She cackled with delight at this unexpected twist in our adventure. I got in last, yanking the door farther open than any of them, thanks to my girth. I wrestled my way inside and pulled the door shut. I tugged on both ropes, in the front seat and in the back.

"Mission accomplished," I said.

"Famous last words," Mark replied.

"We'll get this home," Joseph said. "It's not far, and Dad's gonna drive slow. Right?"

I nodded to Joseph. I appreciated the tactful reminder. To be safe, I probably shouldn't go faster than ten miles per hour. I started the car, backed out of the parking spot, and began to make our way home.

The car grew quiet. A sense of satisfaction emerged. I remembered that I was feeling happy. All of that changed with one very simple question from Macy.

"Daddy, who were those old people in that really big car?"

17

"WHAT OLD PEOPLE?" I said to Macy, speaking to her through the rearview mirror that hung over the dashboard.

"I don't know. The old people. They had a big car. It looked old, too."

"Macy, you didn't see anything like that," Joseph snapped.

"I did, too," she said. "Who were they, Daddy?"

I didn't know where to take this. Joseph hadn't seen them. And if they were there, they hadn't been there for very long. As best I could tell, they'd disappeared nearly as quickly as they'd arrived.

"They're people I know," I said to Macy, uttering the words carefully. "Did you see where they went?"

"They drove away," she said. "Didn't you sthee them drive away?"

"Macy, stop making things up," Joseph said. The edge in his voice fell somewhere between frustration and something that seemed almost a little like fear.

"I'm not making it up. I sthaw them. Daddy, did you sthee them?"

"I saw them," I said to Macy, and I gave Joseph a loaded glance aimed at getting him to let it be. "I saw them."

"I waved to the lady," Macy said. "She waved back."

"Actually, they were at our house last night. During the party."

I saw Macy's eyes widen from inside the mirror. "They were?"

"Dad," Joseph said.

"Yep. They were. They sat on the couch. I got them some food."

"Did they have fun, Daddy?"

"I think they did. But then they left."

"They sure leave fastht."

"They sure do," I said. "They definitely do."

I could sense Joseph glaring at me. I knew he was wondering why I'd be filling Macy's head with such nonsense. But how was that any worse than the annual tall tales of St. Nick? Especially since this one found at least some credence in a cold, hard truth.

Even if no one else saw them, I did. Macy did, too.

Before I knew it, we were home. The boys helped me disconnect the tree from the car.

We carried it inside. They propped it against the wall next to the fake one we'd had for years. I gestured with my chin to the dining room. They knew what to do. After unplugging the lights from the sockets on the wall next to the base of the "B" tree, they gingerly lifted it, moving it slowly and somehow keeping most of the ornaments in place. A couple fell, but Macy scooped them up and held them in her arms as she followed her brothers.

I smiled at the sight of it, especially since it had happened without a single order or any actual guidance from me. In a weird sort of way, it showed they'd be OK without me, without parents, with nothing other than their own motivations and aspirations and above all else each other. I felt at once relieved and fulfilled and entirely irrelevant.

I resisted as best as I could any urge to micromanage. They knew what they were doing. I let them do it. The farther they moved away from me with that tree, the more I sensed that these three humans Linda and I had brought into the world would be just fine, no matter what. That everything else was simply details. I both loved and hated whatever it was that I was feeling.

Eventually, the boys returned. Joseph asked about my plans for the tree with the bulb, the expression on his face suggesting we should have chosen something that both was destined to die and would be easier to position in our TV room. I told him I needed to get a steel tub for the new tree, that it was no big deal because I also needed to get lights and ornaments and whatever else we'd use to decorate the thing that Linda specifically said she wanted for Christmas.

The boys seemed to have no interest in the next leg of the journey, but Macy was ready to do whatever needed to be done to finish the real tree—even if it meant trudging through a blizzard to the North Pole and back again. Buster also wanted to join us. Then again, Buster was always ready to take a ride in the car, right up until the point where he realized he'd be ending up inside the building next to the place where we'd just bought a Christmas tree.

Linda's SUV wasn't in the garage when we'd returned. I didn't know where she'd gone. I knew there was a good chance she'd get back before Macy and I returned with everything we needed to finish the tree. I wanted to surprise her, but Linda already knew we were getting a tree. If she happened to see it propped against the wall with no lights or ornaments and a giant clot of roots and dirt below the branches, so be it.

Still, the sooner we went, the sooner we'd return with the finishing touches for our real, live tree. I wanted to hear more from Macy about what she'd seen in the seconds before and after I'd thrown up all over the parking lot. I also had a strange, gnawing sense that, wherever we ended up, we'd see them again. It gave me a little comfort to know I'd be accompanied by someone who apparently was capable of seeing them, too.

Macy reacted with unrestrained euphoria at the news she'd be the only one of the three siblings to join me for the next leg of our day-before-Christmas-Eve adventure. She bolted for the garage and the backseat of the Subaru before her brothers could change their minds. But they were already back downstairs playing whatever video game they'd constantly been playing, with flimsy headsets strapped to their scalps as they said whatever it was they said while doing whatever it was they did.

Every generation experiences that disconnect, in some way. Something the kids thoroughly understand and their parents utterly do not. Joseph, Mark, and Macy would go through the same thing in their own time. I wondered whether I'd be around to nod knowingly as they expressed their own sense of bewilderment regarding whatever it was that their kids had become mysteriously obsessed with.

I held off Buster's desire to tag along, tail wagging and limbs flailing at the possibility of scrambling into the garage and hopping into the car. Pulling the door shut while fending off the dog (and avoiding another shot to the crotch), I yelled to the boys that we'd be back soon, knowing they either couldn't hear me or wouldn't listen.

I saw the cat when I turned. He was on the shelf, tilting his head in that familiar way. Silently regarding me as a poor bastard who lacked the freedom to find a comfortable spot to hunker down and do nothing at all for the rest of the day.

I didn't mind. I had a purpose, a direction, a mission. The hardest part was done. Or at least I thought it was.

I climbed into the Subaru. Macy sat there, rocking in the back seat with glee. "Where are we going, Daddy?"

"To get everything we need for our new tree," I said. She squealed with raw delight. It was a sound I'll never forget for as long as I live, and hopefully beyond.

Off we went, heading toward the center of all local commercial activity in our town, the rows of big boxes that sold anything and everything that any family in the area would ever need for whatever it was they hoped to do, from filling kitchens and pantries to, for us on that specific trip, finding anything and everything we needed to transform the overgrown weed with a misshapen clump of stuff in a burlap sack into the one specific thing that Linda had said she wanted on this one specific Christmas.

As I backed the Subaru out of the driveway, I realized I'd lost track of time. The clock on the dashboard told me that it was twenty-two minutes past three. We'd have all of it by dinnertime, ideally, and we'd spend the night trimming our new tree.

"We got a great Christhmasth tree, Daddy," Macy said to me. "Mommy will love it."

"It's not ready yet. But it will be."

She ignored those details. "It'sth a great Christhtmasth tree," she said. "I want everyone to sthee it. It will be stho beautiful. Can we get those lightsth that are all different colors?"

"Mommy likes white lights."

"The other tree has white lightsth," she said. "Those are boring. I want all the other colors. She will like them. I sth-wear, she will."

I smiled at that. I nodded. "OK," I said. "We'll get all the other colors."

"Yesth!" she said, and she let out another one of those squeals that hopefully would carry me through whatever the rest of this Christmas and everything after it might hold.

We began making our way to the rows of stores. I turned on the radio and turned up the volume, allowing Christmas music to fill our ears.

"It will be a good Christmas," I said to her.

"Every Christhmasth is a good Christhtmasth," she said.

It would be the forty-sixth one for me. I found myself wondering how many more I'd have. But the only one that mattered was this one. That sense hardened into a firm resolve as we drove, listening to Vic Damone singing *Silver Bells*.

"Can we invite them for Christhmasth?" Macy said.

"Who?"

"Those old people," she said. "They stheem lonely."

"Which old people?" I said, knowing the answer to the question as I asked it.

"Those old people we sthaw when we got the tree, Daddy. Can we invite them?"

"I don't know who they are, honey."

"But they know usth," she said. "I can tell they do. Can you call them?"

"I don't know their phone number."

"Maybe we'll sthee them. If we sthee them, we can invite them. Right, Daddy?"

I told her we would. I didn't know whether we'd see them again, but it seemed like, no matter where I went, they'd be there.

So, yes, we'd invite them. And maybe the rest of the family would finally see them, too. It was nice that Macy had seen them. It would be even nicer if Linda or the boys would see them.

Whoever they were.

18

IT WASN'T QUITE a gesture of reconciliation to U-Sav-Plentee. I just needed some stuff, and I knew I could get it there. So I decided we'd go straight to the local superstore. Yes, I was temporarily suspending my refusal to shop there out of selfishness. I knew it would have everything we needed in order to finish the tree, from the steel tub to the lights to the ornaments to whatever else we'd throw onto it to whatever we'd choose to stick atop its uppermost branch.

Would I get scattered dirty looks from managers I'd questioned in Sandy Matherson's case, or in any other lawsuits I'd handled against the corporate behemoth that treated far too many of its employees like bubonic bedbugs? If I would ever manage to avoid that type of reaction, surely it would occur during the final countdown to Christmas.

As far as I knew, Macy wasn't aware of my ongoing beefs with U-Sav-Plentee. As far as I knew, she was generally aware that I help people who have trouble at work. That's exactly what I believed until I pulled into the parking lot next to the building with the oversized green stripe along the top and the giant sign that had a cascade of neon dollars coming from the letters U, S, and P.

Macy's glee disappeared when she realized where we'd stopped. "I thought you sthaid you'd never buy anything from those dickheads."

"Macy," I said. "I never said that."

"But I heard you tell Mommy. You sthaid the you-sthave-plenty is a bunch of dickheads and you'd never buy anything from them."

"I think you must have been dreaming."

She became quiet for a few seconds. "Daddy, what's a dick-head?"

"It's not a word young ladies should be saying."

"But you sthaid it."

"I'm not a young lady. And I didn't say it. I think you were dreaming."

"How would I dream of a word I never heard before?"

Great, I thought. Yet another lawyer in the family. Maybe the dementia would set in before they got old enough to completely outfox me. For now, I knew how to change the subject.

"I bet they have one of those big bubble gum machines inside. Do you want a gum ball?"

"Yesth! Yesth!" She swung her door open, not looking to see whether other cars were coming. I called for her to wait and scrambled out to grab her.

Along the way, I remembered the keys but I forgot my phone.

I reached for her hand. She grasped my palm with her tiny, little fingers. I remembered having the boys reach an age when they refused to do it. I wondered whether I was already in the final months or weeks until Macy decided (or one of her friends told her) she was too old to hold her father's hand. I squeezed tight at the thought of what would be happening, sooner or later.

"Ouch, Daddy," she said as we walked toward the doors. Just outside, a skinny man stood by the Salvation Army kettle, ringing a bell with mild disdain. He wore a cheap Santa hat and white beard he'd yanked all the way down to the bottom of his chin.

Something about the guy looked familiar. He caught me staring at him. He made a face. It wasn't festive. I kept going without a word or a nod.

Once inside, a greeter rolled a cart in our direction. Macy wanted to ride inside it. I said she couldn't. She didn't push back, for a change. Too bad this whole naughty-and-nice thing didn't hover over them all year long.

It then became wild-goose-chase time. I hadn't entered a U-Sav-Plentee in years. If I ever knew the store's layout, I'd long since forgotten it. I could see in the distance to our left an area that screamed out Christmas. I decided to find the steel tub first, since none of the other things mattered if we couldn't get the tree to stand up straight.

I wanted to find the steel tubs by myself, because I always wanted to find things by myself. But also because I didn't want to talk to any of the employees, to possibly bump into someone I knew from one of my cases.

There was a chance I wouldn't remember them. They definitely would remember me. And I didn't want to risk the kind of conversation that might prompt Macy to blurt out, "Daddy, is thisth one of the dickheads?"

Macy didn't ask questions or complain while I rolled the cart aimlessly, peering down aisles with more people crowded into them than I'd expected to see. Then again, low-low-low prices never sleep.

We found the hardware section. I felt hopeful that, if we were hunting Easter eggs, someone would be saying I was getting warmer.

I turned down one of the aisles. Macy looked at the racks.

"Daddy, I think we have a hammer at home."

"We do, honey. I'm looking for something to put the tree in. Remember, it has that bulb on it?"

"Oh yesth," she said. "And we will plant it after Christhtmasth. Daddy, will the ground be too cold for planting?"

I smiled at that one. She was smart. Smarter than I was at that age. I flinched at a vision of practicing law with her someday. Someday might only be twenty years away. Given how fast the past two decades had flown by, I could blink my eyes and we'd be collaborating on how to force *those dickheads* at U-Sav-Plentee to do right by one of our clients.

"Why are you sthmiling, Daddy?"

"I was just thinking of something, Macy."

"Sthomething funny?"

"Yes, honey. Something funny."

"I like funny things. They're stho, well, funny." She punctuated her profound thought with a shrug, a signature movement of her shoulders that would probably never change, no matter how old she was.

It made me happy. It made me sad.

I turned back to the quest for a steel tub. I noticed what seemed to be a collection of them up ahead, in the next aisle. I started pushing the cart a little faster.

"Daddy, I sthee them."

"Yes, honey, the steel tubs are right up there."

"Not that," she said. "Over there."

I looked at her face. She was turned to the right, her thick glasses showing me the way. I followed the path. I felt my eyes widen.

She did indeed see them, again. Both of them. Roughly thirty feet away from us.

The old man, same black fedora on his head and same brown overcoat covering most of his body, pushing a cart in little spurts. Like ours, it was empty. His wife inched along next to him. They both seemed so small. I wondered whether they could see over the top of the handle.

"Hi!" Macy said, calling out to them. "Hi!"

They didn't react to her voice. They kept moving, feet barely coming off the ground, if at all. They seemed to be talking about something. Almost bickering, the way couples who have been together for decades often do.

"Hello," I said. They heard me, but they didn't seem to be startled, at all. They both turned, smiles instantly brightening faces that radiated through the wrinkles and the loosened flesh. They watched and waited for us to get closer to them.

"I wondered when you'd get here," the old man said.

"You never said that," his wife said.

"I don't say out loud every single thing I'm thinking," he said without turning to her. "Unlike one of us."

She rolled her eyes at him, and I laughed a little bit. Macy broke free from me and rushed toward them. She was almost as tall as the woman.

"Hi," she said to them. "I'm Macthy."

"We know who you are, Macy," the woman said. "You are so beautiful."

The filter between my brain and my mouth failed to catch my next thought. "How do you know who she is?"

"We saw her when you were buying your tree," the woman said, a matter-of-fact tone that might as well have included the word *dumbass* on the back end. "She waved to me. I waved to her."

"How do you know her name?"

"She just told us," the old man said. "Do you need to get your ears checked, too?"

"We're getting a sthteel tub for our tree," Macy said. "It has a bulb stho that we can plant it in the ground after Christhtmasth. But it doesn't sthtand up too good. We have to put it insthide a sthteel tub."

"I bet it will be beautiful," the woman said to her. "Maybe even almost as beautiful as you."

"Will you come sthee it when it'sth ready?" Macy said to them. "Daddy sthaid you were at our housthe."

"You told her we were there?" the old man said to me.

"I didn't know it was a secret."

"Not a secret," he said. "It's something. But I suppose it's not a secret."

"Are you Christhtmasth shopping?"

"Oh, honey, our Christmas shopping is finished."

"Are you getting food for Christhtmasth dinner?"

"No, we don't need any food," she said.

"Well, why do you have a cart then?"

The old man smiled at her. "They gave it to us when we came in."

That both satisfied and amused Macy. She laughed. It made both of them smile more broadly than ever.

"You've done pretty well," the old man said to me.

I jerked my head a bit, dumbfounded by the remark. "Thanks," I replied.

"Other than that pathetic car of yours, that is."

"It'sth a Sthubaru," Macy said. "I'm not old enough to sthit in the front stheat yet."

"You make her sit in the back?" the old man said. "Like a dog or something?"

"Well, you know. The air bags are in the front."

"Air bags?" the old man said.

"He's being simple," the woman said. "Our car doesn't have them."

"Your car is sthooooo huge," Macy said.

"We'll have to take you for a ride," the old man said. "*I'll* let you sit up front."

"Can I, Daddy? Can I ride up front in their huge car?"

"Not right now, Macy. We have shopping to do."

"Later then? Can I ride up front in their huge car later?"

"Maybe," I said.

She shook her head before confiding in her new allies. "Maybe means no," she told them.

"Maybe means maybe, Macy," I said.

"So can they come sthee our Christhtmasth tree?"

She had boxed me into a corner with that one, knowing I wouldn't play the *maybe* card twice in a row. "Sure," I told her. "If they want to. If they can."

"Why couldn't we?" the old man said.

"You told me you're on your way home."

"We are," he said.

"So that means?"

"It means we'd love to see your tree," his wife said. "When should we come?"

"How about Christhmasth dinner?" Macy said to them. "Come to our house for Christmasth dinner."

"Macy, I don't—"

"We'd love to," the old man said, and his wife nodded as he spoke, still beaming at Macy.

That's when I heard another voice, from my left. Away from our conversation. "Is there anything I can help you find?"

I turned. Standing there in a green U-Sav-Plentee vest stretched apart by a midsection that screamed out for the next larger size was a man with a face I instantly recognized. The name tag spelled out DUSTIN in thick, capital letters.

He was one of the assistant managers I'd grilled for ninety minutes just a few days earlier about the rules Sandy Matherson supposedly had broken before she was fired. He had a joyless expression on his face. Flat, dull. Not openly hostile, but I could sense he knew who I was, and that he wanted to politely ask me to get the hell out of his store.

"We're fine," I said.

"I thought you might need some help, since you've been standing here for a while."

"We were having a conversation," I said to him.

He looked at Macy, then he looked back at me. "A conversation? That's a strange way to describe talking to a little girl."

"Not with her," I said, and when I turned back to gesture toward the old man and his wife they were gone. "They were just here."

"They who?" all-caps Dustin said, brow furrowed and expression melting from neutral to skeptical.

"I told you they leave fastht, Daddy."

19

I ROLLED THE cart toward the steel tubs. I picked one that seemed to be large enough for the bulb, but without being too big. I slid it into the space under the basket of the cart, nestling it snugly and firmly into place. We turned toward the Christmas section, the green and red and sparkly and shiny oasis that called out to anyone and everyone who entered the store.

The shelves and racks were full, given how close it was to Christmas. I knew that they never put the current year's items on sale once the holidays came and went. They just crammed it all into one of the large steel containers taking up crooked and random spots behind the store (the manager and his girlfriend used to rendezvous inside one of the containers, according to Sandy Matherson), waited ten months, and sold it at full price the next holiday season.

We started grabbing everything we needed. I didn't worry about getting too much. Their prices really were low. If I ended up with extra, we'd just put it in the attic. Besides, I didn't want to come back here or go to any other store, if I ended up without enough to finish the tree.

Macy held me to the promise of multicolored lights. She snatched five packs of them and dropped them into the cart. Next, she started raiding ornaments filled to the top of clear plastic containers. She got one of each. For some, she grabbed two, whether she meant to or not. She'd say, "Mommy will like thisth one" or "Joseph will like thisth one" or "Buster might eat thisth one if it'sth too low on the Christhmasth tree."

She'd forgotten all about our encounter with the old man and his wife. She didn't even mention it after we noticed they'd essentially disappeared. Her young brain processed things as they were, without questioning how, for example, a pair of elderly people who were roughly the size of emperor penguins and who moved like molasses creeping down a frozen sliding board had high-tailed it out of sight in the short time that I had been interrogated by green-vested, all-caps Dustin.

I, on the other hand, couldn't quit thinking about them. Who were they? And why did it seem as if only Macy and I could see them? They're so small that they're easily missed, I told myself. But that didn't explain Joseph not noticing their U-boat on wheels, I reminded myself.

They were at the house, I thought. I saw them, I insisted. I gave them food, I remembered. I saw them eat it, I knew.

Then they were gone. And the plates I had fixed for them were still sitting on the coffee table, with the food I had gathered and arranged still there, unconsumed.

Someone else had put them there, I told myself. How different of a configuration of the various choices could there have been? You get a little of everything, and you plop it onto a round dish. It wasn't a Monet.

I thought of the other times I'd seen the old man since the

prior morning. I felt my face brighten, and I snapped my fingers. Macy's head jerked in the direction of the sound. Then she tried to mimic the gesture. She held her hand close to her glasses, digging her eyebrows together as her thumb and middle finger struggled noiselessly against each other.

"I can't make a sthnap," she said. "Daddy, will you teach me how to make a sthnap?"

I told her I would. I reached toward the back pocket of my jeans, patting the material on each side in search of my phone. I remembered I'd left the thing in the car. I muttered a curse word, not as quietly as I thought I had.

Macy stopped trying to make a snap. She shot an index finger toward me. "Sthwear jar, Daddy."

"Do we have everything?" I said.

She shifted her attention to the cart, eyes skittering over and around everything we'd piled into it. "I think stho. I think we got lotstha good sthtuff for our Christhtmasth tree."

I spun it around and started for the bank of checkout lines. I wanted to get to the car and make the phone call that maybe would help solve my mystery. Macy tried to get me to use one of the self-service lines. I didn't need to remind her that we like to help keep people employed; I simply told her we had too many things in the cart to do it ourselves.

Ten spots with actual cash registers and conveyor belts remained. Six of them had lights on and cashiers present. I looked at the lines, and I made a guess as to which one would get us checked out the fastest. Number Three was the winner.

I made sure I had my wallet in one of my front pockets. I was pissed at myself for forgetting my phone. Macy was singing, over and over again, the "pa-rum-pum-pum-pum" line from *The Little Drummer Boy*. After the fourth or fifth time she sang it, I started to ask her to stop. But I didn't. It wasn't because I made the conscious decision not to. I just didn't.

"Pa-rum-pum-pum-pum," she continued, rocking her head back and forth while running her eyes up and down and all around the ornaments she'd collected in the basket of the cart.

The customer in front of us, a woman with a vibe that cried out nicotine, worry, and paycheck-to-paycheck dug through an overstuffed purse in search of a rectangular case. She thumbed through various plastic cards. She pulled one out and stuck into the small box across from the cashier.

I could tell she wasn't sure how it would turn out. She shook her head. She tried another card, going through the same routine. After two more, she let out a loud sigh and looked up at the ceiling.

"I'm sorry," she said in a soft voice to the cashier. "I can put everything back."

"What'sth happening, Daddy?"

I shook my head toward Macy, hoping she'd know to let it be. Of course, she didn't. But at least she knew to whisper, even if she hadn't quite perfected the skill of whispering in a way that couldn't be heard by someone who was standing about five feet away from us.

"Does that lady have no money, Daddy?"

I shook my head as slightly as I could, hoping the woman hadn't heard Macy. I feared she did.

"What'sth she gonna do, Daddy?"

I stopped shaking my head and made a quick shrug at Macy. She turned her attention back to the woman.

"That lady looks sthad, Daddy."

I acted like I didn't hear that one. I started to back out of the space between the racks of candy and tabloids so that the woman could pull her cart away and put the stuff she currently couldn't afford to buy back on the shelves.

"How much money does that lady need?" Macy said, still whispering far too loudly.

I ignored her again and began to pull the cart away.

"Where are we going, Daddy?"

"We need to move out of her way," I said, hopeful that my own whispering would help show Macy the ideal range.

"Can we justht pay for the lady's sthtuff, Daddy? It'sth Christhtmasth, Daddy."

I rolled my eyes at that one, a little too aggressively and noticeably. Especially since the woman was starting to pull her cart backward and was now looking right at us.

"Please, Daddy? I'll pay you back with my Christhtmasth money from Grandma and Grandpa."

I stopped. Linda's parents would stuff a one-hundred-dollar bill into Macy's card, same as they did every year with the three kids. Linda always put the money in their college funds. I'd tell Linda that the kids should be allowed to spend the money on whatever they wanted to spend it on. I always lost that argument. The year before, I took them to the mall and told them we were spending their money from Grandma and Grandpa, even if that money was coming from my own pocket. Macy was already looking forward to this year's *shopping sthpree*. I couldn't ignore her willingness to give it up, no matter how badly I wanted to.

"Excuse me," I said to the cashier. "How much is it?"

The woman froze. She was confused by my question. The cashier seemed perplexed as well. "Fifty-seven dollars and twenty-seven cents," the cashier said.

"We'd like to pay it," I said.

I tried not to look at the woman. I didn't want to notice her face as it wrestled with shame on one hand and necessity on the other. She started to sputter and stutter. She said she really couldn't take our money. But she didn't stop me from slipping past her and putting my own credit card into the machine. I punched in all the right numbers, followed all the directions, removed it, and turned to the woman.

"Merry Christmas," I said to her.

"I can pay you back," she said.

"I'm paying for it," Macy said, far too loudly. "With my Christhtmasth money."

The woman turned to Macy and smiled. Macy looked like she wanted to burst with pride and delight. "Thank you," the woman said to Macy.

"You're welcome, lady. Merry Christhtmasth."

The woman nodded. She was fighting back tears. I couldn't tell whether they were tears of joy or sadness or despair or a renewed faith in humanity or some combination of every one of those feelings, and more. At that point, I didn't care. I just wanted to get to the car and make my phone call.

I started pulling ornaments from the basket and dropping them onto the conveyor belt. I was careful not to break any of them, but I still wanted to get this over with. Macy swung around to the back of the cart to help me. We loaded each of the items on the path to the cash register, working to keep up with the cashier.

We'd soon removed all ornaments from the cart. I lifted the flat boxes of multicolored lights and handed them to the cashier, one at a time. After everything we purchased had been listed on the screen across from the cashier's face, I put the same credit card back in the box and paid for all of it. A kid was putting our things in bags and putting the bags in our cart. I helped him finish up.

After we had it all, I began to push the cart toward the exit. Toward the Subaru. Toward my phone.

The cart rolled fast. For a change, I'd gotten one without

that funky wheel that never wants to work right. Macy hurried to keep up with me as we got closer to the doors, the lot, the car, my phone.

"Excuse me," a voice said as we approached the exit. "Hey! Excuse me!"

I stopped. I turned. All-caps Dustin stood there, arms crossed over the green vest that didn't quite fit him. "What's the problem?" I asked.

"I could prosecute you for shoplifting. And maybe I will."

"Shoplifting?" I said. "What are you talking about? I paid for everything. I even paid for everything the woman in front of me bought." I started pushing the cart again.

"Not everything," all-caps Dustin said, this time even louder. "You forgot something. Down at the bottom."

I looked down and saw the steel tub. "Yes, I forgot about that," I said. "I'm sorry."

"Every shoplifter is sorry when he gets caught."

"I didn't mean to do it. I didn't intend to do it. It was an accident."

All-caps Dustin closed in on me, his arms still jammed against the outside of his green vest, his stomach still pressed against the inside of it. "Why don't we let the judge and the jury figure it out?" he said, snarling just a little bit. "That's how you like things to be done, right? Maybe you'd like to see how that feels when it happens to you."

I forced myself to stay calm, especially with Macy standing there, taking in everything that was happening before her widened eyes. "This is not wise," I said to him. "This is not prudent. I made a mistake. I'm happy to pay for it. I want to pay for it. I forgot to pay for it. Do you really want someone's memory of Christmas to include her father getting arrested on some bullshit charge?"

"Sthwear jar," she said in a way that proved she'd already mastered the art of whispering.

"See what you did, Dustin? You made me swear in front of my daughter. Two days before Christmas. That's on you. Now, I'll gladly get back in line and pay for this steel tub. Why don't you let me do that, and then we can go on our way and all of us can enjoy the holidays?"

I couldn't tell whether any of what I'd said had worked. His forearms stayed pressed across his vest. "Enjoy the holidays?" he said. "Do you realize how many people who work in this store have to sweat out the holidays because of you and your client?" He uttered his last word with a sneer, contempt oozing from it.

"My client has rights. Those rights were violated. If anyone is sweating about that, they deserve to."

"Well, maybe you deserve to sweat, too. You're the shoplifter."

"I. Wasn't. Shoplifting," I said, instantly loud enough for anyone within fifteen feet of us to hear it. "Now, if you want to have me arrested on a bogus charge and suffer the consequences for it, go ahead. Otherwise, let me get back in line and pay for the thing I forgot was under my cart. Do we understand each other, Dustin?"

I could feel many eyes on us. I liked it, because I could tell Dustin didn't. He looked down at the steel tub, even as his arms were still criss-crossed over his vest.

"I'll tell you what," he said. "The tub's on the house. You have yourself a merry little Christmas."

I felt my face contorting at the possibility this was some sort of trap, that he was giving me a green light in order to set me up for a swarm of Barney Fifes who'd take me straight to the station and Macy directly to child services. But I felt her tugging on the sleeve of my sweatshirt so I went, trusting it wasn't some ruse. That I wouldn't spend the night before the day before Christmas in a holding cell.

"Thank you," I said, forcing a smile as best I could while pushing the cart away. All-caps Dustin glared at me in response, still standing there with his thick forearms draped across his green vest.

"Don't get cute," he said, "or I might just change my mind."

I resisted the temptation to call his bluff, but only because of Macy. An awkward scene easily could have turned ugly. It didn't, and for that I felt gratitude. I wasn't sure to whom or to what the feeling should be directed, but I felt it nonetheless.

The cart rolled toward the Subaru. I popped the lid open and lifted the bags into the trunk. Macy helped, even if her contribution was to move only one of the bags while I got the rest. After we emptied the basket, I pulled the steel tub from under the cart and slid it into the trunk, pushing some of the bags out of the way.

"We got a free sthteel tub," Macy said, not asking a question or expressing delight but making a flat, objective statement.

"Yes, we did," I said. "We also did a nice thing for that woman. That was all your idea."

"It'sth Christhtmasth," Macy said. She nodded as the lid closed on the back end of the Subaru, a simple and clear acknowledgement of what she'd done.

I smiled at her. "Let's go decorate our tree."

"Yesth!" she said, thrusting her bony arms into air that was becoming much cooler as the sun crept away from view behind hills off in the distance. "Yesth!"

After I helped her inside the back seat, I climbed into my spot. I noticed my phone, and I remembered what I wanted to do.

I picked it up, flashed it in front of my face to unlock it, and pulled up my contacts. Within a matter of seconds, I'd pressed the phone number for Lou Rizzoli.

"Oh," he said, "it's you."

"Merry Christmas to you, too."

"I ain't real happy with you, John."

"I'm sorry, Lou. For whatever I did."

"You know what you did."

"What did I do?"

"You wasted my cousin's time."

"No I didn't."

"Yes. You did. He took his wrecker to the spot to change that tire. There wasn't no one there. No Chevy. No people. No nothing."

I could feel the phone sliding down my cheek as I stared through the windshield at nothing in particular.

"John?" he said. "Hello? John?"

"Tell him I'm sorry," I said. "Tell him to bill me for his time."

As I pulled away, I saw in the rearview mirror the guy who was still manning the Salvation Army kettle. I could have sworn he was staring at me in the reflection. I had more than enough mysterious strangers in my life at the moment to even begin to give it a second thought.

Before I turned away, I noticed something sparkle above his eyebrow.

20

WHEN I NEXT opened the door of the Subaru, I smelled pork chops cooking on the stove. Some aromas are pleasing. Others aren't.

Pork chops weren't one of my favorite dishes from Linda's fairly limited menu. It was an acquired taste I hadn't fully acquired. My main goal whenever she made them was to not end up going to the dentist to have a broken tooth or two fixed.

Macy kept singing "pa-rum-pum-pum-pum" throughout the ride home. I managed to resist the urge to ask her to try a different song, or perhaps to give silence a try. I guess I was reluctantly surrendering to the season. If nothing else, the singing kept me from thinking about whatever was waiting for me on the other side of December 25.

Macy flew out of the back seat and went straight for the trunk. She jumped up and down as it opened. She started grabbing bags of lights and ornaments. I went for the steel tub, since the decorations wouldn't matter until we got the real tree properly positioned. I started inside with determination and focus. I opened the door to the kitchen. The dog came at me again. I spun, avoiding what would have been the second Buster nut buster of the day.

I looked back and noticed the cat, hunkered down in his spot on the shelf. He seemed to be even more disinterested than usual. Yes, I often found myself envying that damn cat.

I yelled for the boys. Macy rushed with some of the bags from the trunk toward Linda. The loose plastic made that loud, screechy sound as Macy opened them. It didn't keep me from hearing Macy, who rattled off to Linda the various things we'd bought at U-Sav-Plentee. I could hear her going on and on, pausing through a spray of lisps to take a breath.

I walked into the TV room and decided where best to drop the steel tub. I looked at the sack full of roots and dirt and wondered whether gravity would really do the trick. Macy kept jabbering, even though I couldn't make out what she was saying.

Then Linda said something; I heard it clearly. "*Who* did you invite to Christmas dinner?"

I stopped what I was doing and listened.

"The old people," I heard Macy say. "They sthaid they were here at the party lastht night. They stheem nicthe. They stheem lonely."

I tried to act like I wasn't paying attention to the exchange while waiting to be involved in it, inevitably.

"Did you know about this?" I heard Linda call from the kitchen.

"Know about what?" I lied, if only to buy a little time.

I heard Linda coming toward the family room, the sound of her footsteps making her disposition clear. "These strangers she invited to Christmas dinner," she said.

"They're not strangers."

"They're strangers to me. I don't know who they are. And I don't know why they were here last night. I'm still not even sure they were."

"Do you think I was lying?" I said.

"I don't know. You play stupid jokes sometimes. You had some wine last night. I know how you get when you've had a stressful week and then you drink a little. I've seen it. But I sure didn't see them."

"Well, I saw them last night. And I saw them today. Macy saw them, too."

"How am I supposed to fit two more people at the table? We have just enough spots for everyone."

"What about the kids' table?"

"It's the kids' table."

"Well, they're basically the same size as the kids. And Macy likes them. They seem to like her."

"Right, John. I'm going to put two elderly strangers at the table with our kids and my sister's kids for Christmas dinner. Maybe their dentures will fall out onto the table while they're eating."

"Not as long as you don't serve pork chops."

"Excuse me?"

I backed away from the metal contraption that had almost gotten me thrown in jail before we got it at a one-hundred-percent discount. "It'll be fine," I said. "They won't show up."

"They showed up last night, according to you."

"So what if they do? It's Christmas. Macy's right. They seem lonely. What's wrong with giving two lonely old people a meal on Christmas Day?"

"But who are they?"

"I don't know. I'd never seen them before yesterday. But I keep running into them."

"Running into them? Where?"

I moved closer to Linda. I tried to read her. After all these years, sometimes she was as much of a mystery to me as she was the first time I'd met her. "Look, we didn't get a chance to talk yesterday. I saw that old man three different times. And that was before they showed up here. When I was driving to court, they had a flat tire on the side of the road. I stopped to help them."

"I have a hard time picturing you changing a tire."

"I know how to change a tire."

"So did you?"

"No. I had to get to court. I made a phone call and had someone go out there and help them." I didn't mention that the someone who showed up to help couldn't find them.

"Where else did you see them?"

"They were parking next to my car on the street. The old man thought he'd hit my bumper. If he did, he didn't leave a mark. Then I saw him when I stopped at the grocery store."

"So you invited him here last night." It wasn't a question.

"I didn't. I didn't even tell him my name. I have no idea how or why they showed up last night."

She studied my face, probing for any sign I wasn't being truthful. Hoping to find anything to confirm the suspicion that I was messing with her. I could tell in the expression on her face that, for a change, she had nothing.

"I know what you're thinking," I said. "But Macy saw them."

"What happened in court yesterday?"

"Do you mean none of your little friends told you last night? I just presumed it would be big news."

"How would my friends know? I just thought you lost and didn't want to discuss it."

"I told you I didn't lose," I said. "At least not yet."

"I still don't know what that means."

"We'll finish after the first of the year. I'll lose then."

"I suppose I need to prepare for your new friends to be here for Christmas. I have enough other things to worry about. I've been busting my ass around here lately. With very little help."

"We'll figure something out. If they show up, we'll find a place for them. It means a lot to Macy."

"I get the feeling it means a lot to you, too."

"I don't know about that. But I do know I'd like to figure out who they are. And I'd love to know why all of a sudden they seem to keep popping up wherever I go."

She kept looking at me. "Why don't you just ask them?"

I felt a smile involuntarily emerging. She was right. I would just ask them. How hard would that be? It was an appropriate question. Why are you showing up everywhere I go? Why did my son not see your gigantic car when it was right there, right in front of us? And what exactly do you want from me?

That was really the most important question.

What exactly do they want from me?

"What do you think of the tree?" I said to Linda.

"It has potential," she said. "Although I would have been fine without buying one that we're going to have to plant. But I assume Macy insisted on getting a tree that we wouldn't just throw away after Christmas."

"She really wanted this tree. What was I supposed to tell her? You should have seen her. I couldn't bring myself to say no to her. Not about that."

Linda seemed to be softening a bit, even though I could tell she didn't want to. I wished I could read her mind.

Or maybe I really didn't want to know everything that was actually going on inside her brain. At least not until after Christmas.

21

I MANAGED TO eat most of one pork chop and part of another without having to arrange for emergency dental care. At that point, I'd take my wins wherever I could find them.

The kids were either oblivious to the dehydrated shoe leather or numb to it. Or maybe they were smart enough to not get Santa's liaison riled up so close to The Big Night. I watched them, dumbfounded by their ability to chew and chomp and swallow without large glasses of milk to soften things up and wash them down.

Macy and I helped clear the table, rinse the plates, fill the dishwasher. Joseph and Mark hustled out of sight and back to the basement, for more of whatever it was they spent so much time playing. I made a mental note to do a little research about the game. If I ever managed to figure out the name of it.

I decided to give it a try with their sister.

"Macy," I said as casually as I could, "what's the game the boys play?"

"It'sth called Sthabotage."

"Sabotage?" I said. The name didn't register. "What do they do?"

"They play it."

"No," I said, "what do they do while they are playing it?"

"I don't know, Daddy. They just sthit there, I sthuppose."

I stopped trying to jam a dish into a spot where it didn't want to fit, while Buster tried to lick from the plates in a way so discreet that he must have thought we couldn't see him doing it.

"I mean what is the game?" I said. "What does the game do?"

"They just go all around and shoot sthtuff," she shrugged. "I don't like those games."

"I don't either," I told her, happy to have gotten the name of the game without pulling her string hard enough to get her to blurt out to them that I was asking a bunch of questions about the game they play. Not that they would have cared.

Linda had slipped away while I was talking to Macy. The kitchen was clean. I double- and triple-checked to ensure I'd gotten everything. I lit a few of the Christmas candles. Officially, I wanted the house to have that full and robust holiday aroma. Unofficially, well, it was high time for the pork-chop smell to be cleared out of the first floor.

I went to the TV room. Macy followed me. We still had work to do. I'd tried before dinner to smush the burlap sack into its new container. The boys helped.

It didn't want to adapt to the shape of the tub. Because of course it didn't. The tree was standing, but it was crooked. A leaning tower of Pisa pine. Maybe it would straighten out as it settled. I had a feeling the chances of that happening before Christmas morning were slim.

"It looksth good," Macy said. She was nodding, as if enough head bobbing would convince her and me that it did. I appreciated that she was trying to make me feel a little better.

"Well, we need to get the lights and ornaments on it, even if it's slanting a little."

"It'sth not sthlanting a little, Daddy."

"That's nice of you to say, honey."

"It'sth sthlanting a lot."

I looked again at the tree. She was right. It *was* slanting a lot. And no amount of decorations would change that. If anything, the influence of gravity on the ornaments would make it more clear. But it was too late to fret about that. This was our tree. Macy wanted to keep it after the holidays. Once planted, it wouldn't be crooked. Unless I found a way to screw that up, too.

"Let'sth put the lightsth on it, Daddy."

That snapped me out of it. I began busting open boxes and pulling cords and ultimately wrapping lights around and around and around. We put six strands on the tree. Better to have too many than not enough.

Unfortunately, the lights didn't make it look any less crooked. At least they didn't make it look any more crooked.

We started on the ornaments. It would have been easier if the boys had been helping. But this project had become mine and Macy's. We were the ones who had seen the old man and his wife. We were the ones who would get the tree ready. I was almost looking forward to the old man walking in and making a smart remark.

"Your tree looks nice and straight but the rest of your house sure is tilted."

Macy kept handing me ornaments. I kept hanging them up. From time to time, she'd tell me where to put them. I did whatever she said. I wanted nothing more than for her to remember the year she and her father trimmed the live tree that wouldn't stand up straight, the live tree that would end up living in the backyard for years. Maybe decades. For as long as the family lived in that house, if not a lot longer.

Maybe, in her seventies, she'd tell her spouse to pull the car down the driveway so she could traipse slowly toward the tree and let its needles press against the back of her hand. Maybe I'd be there, somewhere. Watching her. Seeing the glint in her eye. The one that wanted so desperately to rewind back to this moment. The moment we now shared.

"What'sth wrong, Daddy?"

I brushed from my cheek a tear that already was snaking its way toward the jawline I used to have. "Nothing," I said. "I'm just happy."

"Don't cry if you're happy," she said. "Sthmile."

I did. I smiled for a long time, watching her as she kept handing ornaments to me and I kept putting them on the tree. I felt something. An awareness. A calm. Was it spiritual, or even religious? I wasn't much for any of that, despite having it drilled into my brain during a dozen years of Catholic school.

I felt something different. It made me forget about everything that had been going on and to absorb the event with my daughter, fully and completely. It could be the last one we shared like this for a long time. It could be the last one we shared like this, ever.

Buster wandered in from time to time, sniffing around before leaving and then coming back and leaving again. The cat at one point parked on top of the couch and regarded the whole scene with bemusement. Then again, he always looked at us that way.

From time to time I heard a yelp from one of the boys in the basement. They were good about not cursing loud enough for me to hear, even though they'd heard plenty of that talk from me. Thus the swear jar, into which I'd already deposited enough dollar bills to buy a bungalow on a beach somewhere.

We got closer to finishing. It was starting to look good, despite the obvious departure from its intended direction. Macy began to giggle randomly at the sight of it. Her laughter was infectious, contagious. For me at least. The cat continued to be thoroughly unaffected. He'd stay that way until he heard me cranking the can opener the next morning.

The two-man stampede began again, clambering up the stairs, boxing each other out on their way to whatever they'd decided they needed to get from the refrigerator. I called out to them to go easy. It didn't take long for Joseph to yield to his own curiosity, and it didn't take long after that for Mark to decide he might have been missing something.

"How long will it be like that?" Joseph said.

"I don't know," I said. "Hopefully not long."

"Should we tie it to something?" Joseph said.

"It's gonna fall," Mark observed, face aglow from the screen of his phone.

"It's not gonna fall," Joseph said.

"Five bucks says it will."

"Five bucks says you're gonna fall first," Joseph said.

"I've got an idea," I told them. "Maybe we can use some fishing line to prop it up."

I could see Macy's brow furrow behind her glasses. "There's no fish in trees, justht birds," she said.

Joseph nodded and left the room, heading to the garage and tracking down one of the tackle boxes. We didn't fish much, but we did it enough to have the basic gear. And I was pretty sure we had clear fishing line that I could loop around the trunk, tie into a knot, and attach to the window or the wall. It wouldn't be a perfect solution, but it would be good enough while the contents of the burlap sack settled into the steel tub we'd gotten for free from all-caps Dustin at U-Sav-Plentee.

Joseph came bounding back into the TV room, pleased that he'd found the flat plastic spool of eight-pound test. It was clear, as I'd remembered. I never bought fishing line in purple or any other color. The fish still have eyes, I'd reasoned.

I asked Joseph to find a pair of scissors. He rolled his eyes when I reminded him to keep them pointed to the ground and to walk them back in. I knew how it sounded, but the last thing I wanted to do that night (or any night, really) was to make a trip with one of the kids and a bloody towel to the emergency room for a fresh batch of stitches. So far, we'd managed to avoid having to do that with any of them, for any reason. I wasn't about to end our unlikely streak on the eve of Christmas Eve.

I came up with a plan that was hopefully more MacGyver than MacGruber. It was definitely on the low end of low tech. I'd string fishing line around the midpoint of the tree and slide it around the latch in the middle of the window frame. I'd pull it sufficiently tight to straighten out the tree, and I'd twist it all together and triple knot it in place. It would work. Not much had been certain to me that day (or the day before), but I was absolutely certain this plan would work.

Macy watched silently. It possibly was the longest she'd gone without saying a word in days. I sensed from her not necessarily pride but a reaffirmation that maybe her father knew how to get things done.

Before too long, I'd finished. Mark looked up from his phone long enough to see that the tree was now mostly straight. "It's still gonna fall," he said.

Macy turned to him and threw her hands on her hips. "No it'sth not, you dickhead."

"Macy!" I said, swallowing my laughter.

"I know it's a sthwear jar," she said. "But it's our Christhmasth tree. He shouldn't say things like that about it."

"You shouldn't say that, honey. It's not nice."

"He's not nicthe. It's our Christhmasth tree. And now it'sth perfect."

"I don't know about that. But it's a lot better than it was."

She beamed as she looked at it, complete with the lights and ornaments we'd bought. "It'sth perfect, Daddy. Let'sth show it to Mommy."

"I'm not sure where she is," I said.

That became Macy's signal to begin yelling "Mommy!" repeatedly, scurrying toward the stairs and continuing to call it out over and over until Linda came down the steps and entered the TV room.

"Where were you?" I said.

"Upstairs, obviously. What's going on?"

I gestured toward the tree. She looked at it. She smiled. I tried to read whether it was genuine. It was genuine enough for Macy.

"Here's our Christhmath tree, Mommy. You wanted a real Christhmasth tree. And here it is. Daddy made it sthtraight."

"It's beautiful," Linda said to Macy. "Thank you, kids."

They approached her for a hug. I watched the four of them, together. I felt disconnected from the group. I resisted the desire to point out that I'd done plenty of the work, or to say anything else. This time became theirs. I tried to force myself to enjoy it. I still felt isolated and apart from it.

It's fine, I told myself. It's her tree. They're her kids. She'd carried them. She'd given birth to them. They were much more hers than mine. They always would be. It's fine, I told myself again. I had my share with them that day, it was time for Linda to have hers. It was stupid for me to feel whatever I was feeling.

Jealousy? Not really. Separation. Distance. Confusion.

Things were changing. Change was coming. Good or bad or whatever, things were going to be different after Christmas. Things would never be the same as they'd been. I didn't know how or why, but I knew it.

I saw the cat jump off the couch and run out of the room.

22

I SLEPT, RESTLESSLY. Dreaming in visions and voices and nonsense. I woke up twice. Once to pee. Once to sit on the edge of the bed until Linda stirred from her slumber long enough to realize I was awake. She didn't say anything to me.

As daylight began to sneak through blinds I could never get to fully close, I was sleeping more soundly than I had throughout the night. Clinging to the escape from reality during its inevitable final minutes. That day, inevitable came bouncing into the bedroom in the form of Macy and Buster. She moved around to my side of the mattress and got in my face while the dog nudged his snout past her and ran his tongue across the tip of my nose.

"Daddy, wake up," she said, pushing Buster away. She put her palms on the white stubble sprouting from my cheeks. Those little hands felt warm and alive. She patted as gently as she could, which wasn't very gentle at all.

"It's Christhtmasth Eve," she said. "We have kids' break-fastht on Christhtmasth Eve."

My eyes shot open. I'd forgotten the tradition we'd started five years earlier, when Macy was too small to make the trip with the boys and me. We'd go to a short-order local chain for a greasy, nasty, delicious meal that would inch me just a little closer to that coronary, one day before the annual commemoration of Christ's birth. Just like Baby Jesus would want it, or something.

"Are the boys up?"

"Yesth," she said. "They're playing Sthabotage again."

"Are they ready?"

"They're already playing."

"No, I mean are they ready to go?"

"I think stho. I will go tell them."

"Good idea," I said.

She pulled her palms away. I already missed that connection to her. I spun out of bed after Macy rushed away on her new mission, Buster following closely behind.

Quick shower and shave; farewell to the instant St. Nick disguise, just add sleep. I toweled my hair dry and brushed it mostly into place. I used a few blasts of jet wash from a sleek pink contraption Linda apparently had bought while getting her hair done for Christmas. I wasn't quite sure when or where she went. There was a time I'd know little things like that. They came up in basic human conversation, among humans who were close enough to engage in basic conversation. In recent months (or maybe years), she never mentioned when she was going to the salon. I never asked.

I rifled around in the closet for a fresh pair of jeans and a different sweatshirt, clothes that would have enough room to let me enjoy the meal I was about to devour. After the holidays,

I'd be getting my act together. For now, my act would continue to be hopelessly all over the place.

By the time I made it downstairs, Macy had managed to disconnect the boys from their game. It's possible Linda helped the cause with the kind of sharp, stern message that always seemed to work on them. Or anyone, for that matter. Teachers know how to motivate quickly, and it was obvious based on how she ran her household that Linda kept a pretty tight ship in the schoolhouse, too.

We went through the same routine as the day before, everyone assuming the seats they'd taken when we went on our search for a real, live tree. This adventure would be easier. There was a Denny's across from U-Sav-Plentee. I wasn't a big fan of the place, but the kids loved it. Besides, I'd eat whatever they put in front of me, as long as it wasn't moving. Much.

More cars were jammed into the parking lot than I'd expected, especially on Christmas Eve. I remembered it was a Sunday. The ultimate test of the church-every-week crowd came when Christmas landed on a Monday. Only the truest of the true believers would show up for full-blown services on back-to-back days. Based on the struggle to find an empty spot for the Subaru, plenty of people were trying to convince themselves, or at least everyone else, that they were more pious than their peers.

Inside the front doors, I saw a collection of folks of various sizes, shapes, and ages who were waiting for tables. I wandered to the podium. The hostess fought through her default attitude of impatience and frustration and pretended she wasn't irritated at all. Maybe she was acting that way because tomorrow was Christmas. Maybe, for some, annual fear of the naughty list leaves a permanent scar.

"Merry Christmas," she said through a fake smile while

chomping on a wad of gum that flopped around in her mouth like a pink sweater tumbling in a dryer. "How many today?"

"Four," I said, "and one children's menu, please."

The fake smile stayed put as she told me it would be roughly five or ten minutes for a table. Based on the number of people who were waiting, I guessed it would take longer than that. But I wasn't in a rush. Besides, the boys had their phones, and Macy would *pa-rum-pum-pum-pum* her way through the delay.

We found a place to stand, since the seats were mostly occupied. There was a stray open space here and there in the alcove for those who were waiting to be seated. I stood there, hands on Macy's shoulders while the boys remained transfixed by their devices. I tried to keep my eyes on the top of Macy's head, studying the frizz of hair that often seemed to have a mind of its own.

I didn't feel like talking to anyone, other than the kids. I hoped we wouldn't see any of my clients. Especially not Sandy and Earl Matherson. I also didn't want to be noticed by anyone from U-Sav-Plentee, especially none of the employees who had ever been on the wrong side of being aggressively interrogated by me under oath.

"Daddy, Daddy," Macy barked out, pointing a finger through the double glass doors and into the parking lot. "They're here."

I looked up and felt warmth mixed with confusion. There it was. The aircraft carrier on wheels. With a tiny little captain and an even smaller first mate. The Chevy chugged by slowly, under the old man's mostly steady command. I saw the top of his fedora, barely making it above the steering wheel, as usual.

"Can they eat with usth, Daddy?"

"I'm not even sure they're coming in, Macy."

"Earth to Daddy. Why elsthe would they be in the parking lot?"

"Who's in the parking lot?" Joseph said.

"The old people," Macy said. "They are stho nicthe. We sthaw them at the sthtore with those dickheads."

"Macy," I said, tugging on her shoulder.

"You mean the people I didn't see?" Joseph said. "When we got the tree?"

"Same ones," I said. "I guess we'll see if you see them now."

"What's that mean?" Joseph said.

"They're coming!" Macy sprang on the balls of feet tucked into thick white sneakers with red and green laces.

There they were, indeed. The woman led the way. The old man struggled to keep up with her. They looked the same as they always did. I think they were wearing the same clothes every time I saw them.

"I know them," Joseph said.

"Know who?" I asked.

"Them. Those people. They're from our church."

"They are?"

"Mom doesn't make you go. So I think we'd know."

"I never stheen them at our church."

"That's because you're coloring pictures or eating Cheerios," Mark said. I was somewhat surprised that our conversation had broken the spell of his phone.

"Do you recognize them?" I said to Mark.

He pulled his eyes away from the screen long enough to take in the elderly couple creeping toward the door. "They're from our church."

"Told you," Joseph said.

"I never stheen them at our church."

"Be polite to them," I told the boys.

"Why do you think we wouldn't be?"

"I don't know. It's just something to say."

I could feel Joseph's eyes on me as I watched the old couple get closer. "Are you OK, Dad?"

"I'm fine," I said without turning away. "We're fine. Everything's fine."

"I think Dad's losing it," Mark said, eyes glued back to his device.

"I can help you find it, Daddy," Macy said. "What is it?"

"Kids, I said I'm fine. Let's just say hello to these people. Whoever they are."

"Can they sthtill eat with usth?"

I nodded to Joseph, and he got the message to help them inside. He passed through the first set of doors and then beyond the small lobby that kept the cold air out. He opened the outer entrance. He stepped back and away and stood there, waiting for them to walk inside. I couldn't hear what they were saying, but they stopped to admire him. They acted as if they knew him. The old man reached up to pat him on the shoulder, and his wife placed her hand on Joseph's wrist as she came inside.

I nudged Mark, whose head jerked up at me. I motioned with my chin. Once he saw his brother holding the outer door, Mark moved to open the inner one. They stopped to look at him, too.

"Another fine young gentleman," the old man said. "Lucky for you, you don't look much like your father."

"I see the resemblance," the woman said. "Why wouldn't the boy want to look like his father?"

Macy broke free from me and rushed to them, wrapping her arms around the woman's waist and burying her head into the woman's coat. "Merry Christhmath," Macy said. She pulled her face back and looked up at the old man, a distance that was more like inches instead of feet. "Do you want to eat breakfastht with usth?"

"That sounds delightful," the woman said.

"I'm not picking up the check," the old man said from behind his wife, loud enough for me to hear. Probably on purpose.

"It's our treat," I said to them, before his wife could respond.

"Well, then I'll be getting one of everything," the old man chortled.

"Can I get one of everything, too, Daddy?"

"He's joking," the woman said to Macy.

"Speak for yourself," the old man said. "I'm starving." He looked at me. "You know, she doesn't feed me."

Mark and Joseph had returned. I wanted to make the formal introductions. It would be the best and easiest way to get these people to say their names out loud. As I opened my mouth, the gum-chewing hostess kept me from continuing.

"Persepio? Four?"

I turned and walked to the podium before the others could follow. "I actually need six."

"You said four."

"I know I said four. But our plans changed. I need six."

"It's a table for four. I guess we can put one at each end. It could be a little tight."

"It's fine," I said. "We'll make it work."

I turned back to our growing group of breakfasters and motioned for them to come along. I led them toward the empty table. The hostess told a busboy to get two more seats. I watched as he moved toward a wall along the outside of the kitchen. Several extra standard-issue Denny's chairs were stacked on top of each other.

My eyes then strayed to the opening in the kitchen, where the cooks were working over the grill with eggs and bacon and sausage and whatever else they were preparing before dropping the plates onto a metal surface, ready to be picked up and served.

One of the cooks looked familiar. He was skinny, with a ratty mustache. It looked like he had a piercing above his eyebrow. I squinted to see whether it was a metal lighting bolt. I couldn't tell for sure.

I looked away when I noticed him staring at me.

23

CHRISTMAS EVE BREAKFAST gave me plenty to think about on the drive home. When I introduced them to Joseph and Mark, the old couple didn't say who they were. Fortunately, Macy blurted out, "What are your names?" At that point, they had no choice but to come clean. If that's what they actually did.

I saw them glance at each other, sort of nervously but also knowingly. As if they expected to get the question eventually, and they had a plan to deal with it. But who needs a plan when asked a simple question like what do you call yourself?

"We're the Alexanders," she said to us. "I'm Eleanor and this is Roscoe."

Macy had laughed out loud at the sound of the old man's name.

"Yes, it is funny," the woman said to her. "I laughed the same way when he first told me. They used to call him Butch."

Macy's head jerked toward me. "That'sth the cat'sth name!"

she said. She then spun back to them, delighted in the discovery. "Our cat'sth name is Butch!"

"That's quite a name for a cat," the old man said. "I always thought it was more of a dog's name."

"Our dog's name is Busthter," Macy said. "We should have named him Butch."

"That's a fine name, too," the woman said. "Butch and Buster. I can tell you love them very much."

"The cat is weird," Macy said. "But Busthter is my best friend. He sleeps in my bed with me."

We ordered a bunch of things I shouldn't have been eating. I didn't care. Everyone was happy. Even Mark and Joseph, too deep in their phones to join the conversation, seemed pleasant and satisfied, in their own disconnected way. The old man watched them, contentedly. I expected him to pepper them with a bunch of questions about the flat little boxes that were holding their full attention. But he seemed pleased to just take it all in.

He definitely was pleased to have a plate of eggs, bacon, hash browns, and toast dropped in front of him. The woman got the same. I watched them eat the food. The old man had flecks of scrambled egg on his coat (he never took the thing off), and his wife told him to brush them away. He dismissed her with a wave of the hand, but then he did as he'd been instructed.

After we left the table, I went to the cashier to pay the bill. I added the tip to the receipt. I glanced back at the table. I wandered over to it. I wanted to see if their food was really gone. But the table had already been cleared. I noticed something tucked under the salt shaker. It was a hundred-dollar bill, folded in half. It looked old, like the ones they made when I was growing up.

I started to pick it up and look at it. I could feel eyes on me.

I turned around. The cook with the piercing in his eyebrow that may or may not have been a lightning bolt was watching me. I nodded at him. He didn't nod back. I walked away from the table.

I kept thinking about those final minutes of our Christmas Eve breakfast. I finally knew who the old man and the woman were, or at least who they claimed to be. Now I wanted to know who that cook was. He looked so damn familiar. Was he the guy who had sold us the tree? Was he the fake Santa working the Salvation Army kettle outside U-Sav-Plentee? Was he both of them? All of them? Was he maybe a potential client I'd once met at my office but decided not to represent? A witness from an old case? Someone who mowed our lawn or shoveled our driveway?

Or was he working for the brother-in-law of Gary Galloway? It had been only two days since the city employee who'd removed the boot from my car had made a not-so-vague threat. Did he hire this guy to follow me around, to figure out the best time to make a move?

I told myself it sounded stupid. But all of it was stupid. I kept seeing the old couple everywhere I went. Why was it crazy to think this other guy would be showing up in a bunch of different places, too?

I piddled around the first floor of the house that afternoon, thinking through the possibilities while doing some of the various things that needed to be done to prepare for a small Christmas Eve dinner and a larger meal the next afternoon. The one that the Alexanders, or whoever they were, supposedly would be attending.

At first, I doubted they'd show up. Now, I wasn't so sure. Maybe it's because I was no longer sure about anything. Still, Macy had asked them at least five times during breakfast whether they'd be there. Every time, they said yes. The

Alexanders said yes. I kept trying to think of them as the Alexanders. Part of me didn't want to accept that was who they really were.

I also didn't have many rules I followed, but one was to not drink alcohol before dinner, ever. By the middle of the afternoon, I found myself wanting to get a bottle of wine and begin working my way through the first half of it. I vowed to wait to crack it open as Linda began to whip together our Christmas Eve meal.

In the kitchen, I asked whether we should invite her parents for dinner. Her eyes widened.

"You always say family only for Christmas Eve dinner."

"Well, they're family, too."

"That's what *I'm* supposed to say," she said, still dumbfounded by the question.

"I just feel like maybe we should."

"They're going to my sister's, like always."

"They go there every year."

"Yes, John, they go there every year because you always say family only for Christmas Eve dinner."

"Well, maybe I changed my mind."

"It's probably a little too late for that. Besides, I'm not sure I have enough food for them, too. And I've got the ham going for tomorrow. It's not like we have an industrial kitchen here."

"You could at least ask them. Even if they say no, it would be a nice gesture."

"The nice gesture would have been to think of this before right now."

"I'm sorry," I said. "I should have. I've just been preoccupied with work."

"You're still preoccupied. Not with your work, but with something."

"I'm just—I don't know. I guess I'm confused."

"Confused about what?"

"I don't know. It's been a strange few days."

"It's been strange for more than a few days."

"What does that mean?"

"Let's just get through the next couple of days. For the kids. They need that. Kids always remember the Christmases. We owe it to them to make it a good one. We can worry about everything else later."

I didn't like her words or the way she delivered them. I felt shadows creeping over me from every direction. Maybe my obsession with the old man, the woman, the tree salesman/ fake Santa/short-order cook had become my defense mechanism. Or maybe they were part of the problem. If it even was a problem. Maybe it was a solution.

I really wanted that wine. The clock in the microwave said it was five minutes past four. Close enough, I decided. We had plenty for the next day, including several bottles that were more expensive than the usual twist-off stuff we'd buy. I saw one with a label that looked interesting (and that was pretty much all I knew about wine). I began to peel the foil away from the top, so that I could screw out the cork. If I even remembered how to do it.

Linda stayed in the kitchen. I could tell she wanted to question me about choosing to pop open a bottle of wine at least ninety minutes before dinner. She didn't. I wondered whether I wanted her to. Getting the question would at least mean she still cares. Maybe she doesn't. Maybe I don't either.

I got the cork out of the bottle without too much of a struggle. I found a wine glass big enough to hold a long, slow pour, and it got one. I picked it up and stuck my nose over the top, clueless as to what I was supposed to be smelling. But I knew that the contents would help calm me down, just enough to get through dinner and maybe beyond.

I carried the glass of wine to the TV room. I plopped onto the couch. I admired the tree we'd bought and trimmed and found a way to make stand in a way that was mostly vertical. I felt a little burst of pride. Not much, but just enough to distract me from whatever it was that was making me feel whatever I was feeling.

I sipped the wine, letting the warmth enter my throat and my stomach and spread throughout my body. Before too long, it was gone. I made my way back to the kitchen for more. Once again, Linda said nothing about it. I considered chugging it straight from the bottle, if only to see whether she'd react.

Back to the TV room I went. Back to the spot where the old man and woman had, or hadn't, been sitting less than forty-eight hours earlier. Eating while not eating the food I'd gotten for them. I could sense the wine working. My brain relaxed. I kept thinking about the old man and the woman. About the fake Santa tree-selling fry cook. My brain felt like a box full of puzzle pieces that desperately wanted to be put together by someone who knew how to do it. That person apparently wasn't me.

I finished the second glass. I put it on the same table where the old man and the woman had placed empty plates that weren't. I wondered if, when I looked back at the wine glass, it magically would be full again.

I nestled into the couch and shut my eyes. The wine did the rest. By the time sounds of dinner being prepared nudged me awake, it was dark outside. That only made the tree and the lights on it stand out more brilliantly. I felt young again. Not twentysomething young, even though those days were fading deeper and deeper into the past. I felt like a kid again. I felt like I was at home, with my parents and Baby Michael. I felt like I was trapped in one of those holiday scenes that feels like it will last forever. At that moment, I wanted to be.

I thought of the old man and the woman. I sat up on the couch. It can't be. It isn't. I wondered whether my newly-acquired habit of vomiting without warning was the product of a brain tumor, a tumor that also was causing me to hallucinate. With hallucinations so convincing that I had hallucinated my way into thinking Macy had joined me in my delusion.

But the boys had finally seen them. They were a couple from church. A couple Macy hadn't seen in church. Maybe they'd be at midnight mass. Maybe Linda could serve as the ultimate arbiter of who in the hell these people were and why in the hell they kept showing up.

I heard Linda mumbling about something in the kitchen. It was my cue to get up and offer to help. We didn't go for the full-blown seven-fishes Italian feast. She fried cod in a pan on the stove (we all would be stinking of it at church) and made a simple concoction of elbow macaroni and white Northern beans tossed in garlic and onions sautéed in olive oil. My mom used to make it every Friday. My dad hated it. It reminded him of the cheap food they ate when he was barefoot young and dirt poor.

Still not entirely awake, I stumbled into the kitchen. I steadied myself against the surface of the island.

"I can remember when you used to be able to drink a lot more than that before passing out," she said.

"I didn't pass out."

"Sure you didn't."

"What can I do to help?"

"I need to check the ham."

"OK," I said, not quite sure what she would actually be checking on it.

"You can pull it out of the oven and put the pan on top of the stove," she said.

"I can do that," I said, nodding. I opened the door to the oven. It smelled a lot better than her pork chops.

"I'd use oven mitts, if I were you," she said.

"I may be stupid," I said, "but I ain't dumb." She didn't respond at all to what had been one of my sayings from our early years together.

I pulled open a couple of drawers until I found the thick mittens. I put them on and held my hands in the air like a doctor who'd been scrubbed and prepared for surgery. "I'm ready to operate," I said.

Again she didn't respond. "Just don't drop it," she said. "And be careful. It's heavier than it looks."

I grabbed the pan. I lifted it by the handles and placed it on the stove, over a front burner that wasn't occupied. Was it too close to the edge of the stove? In hindsight, I guess it was. That's one of the reasons why they call it hindsight.

I inhaled the aroma. It needed more time to cook, but it was nearly close enough to make me want to grab a knife and slice away a chunk of it.

"Don't think about it," Linda said.

"Don't think about what?"

"Don't think about what you're thinking about. I know that look on your face. That ham is for tomorrow. You can have all you want then."

"That makes me want it even more right now."

Macy appeared in the kitchen. "I sthmell ham. It sthmells so good. Can I have some please?"

"No, Macy," Linda said.

"I sthaid please."

"You always need to say please," Linda replied, "but saying please doesn't always work."

Macy scrunched her nose. "Why can't we have ham tonight? I don't like fish."

"You like fish," I said to her.

"Not as much as I like ham."

"You'll turn into a little ham if you eat too much of it," Linda said.

"Don't say that," I said. "You'll give her a complex."

"What'sth a complexth? I want one."

"No, you don't."

"Do you have one, Daddy?"

"I've got a few. You'll end up with one of them eventually."

"I want one now," Macy said.

"Maybe Santa will bring you one," Linda said.

I flinched a bit at that. Linda liked to try to be funny, but that just seemed like an odd thing to say. I took off the oven mitts and moved around the island. Linda had said she needed to check the ham. I wanted to give her plenty of room to do whatever she needed to do before I put the thing back in the oven.

"What time does Sthanta get here? Will he come when we're at church?"

"He'll wait until after we get home and go to bed."

"But what if he comes to our neighborhood before then?"

"He won't," I said.

"But what if he does?"

"He won't, Macy," Linda said. "You just have to accept that."

I wondered whether this would be the last year for Macy. She was asking too many questions. Figuring out too many holes in the logic. I was both proud and dismayed. Unless we were going to have another kid, and the chances of that fell somewhere between slim and none, it was all about to end. Maybe that was good. I'd never felt comfortable lying about the one thing that served as the centerpiece of a child's existence.

I still remembered figuring it all out when I was six years old. At the time, I didn't care. As long as I was able to open a bunch of presents on Christmas morning, it didn't matter where they came from. If anything, understanding how it all really worked eliminated the middleman, stripped away the mystery. I knew my audience, when it came to putting together my annual list of coveted toys and whatnot. It also wiped out the fear of being under twenty-four-hour secret surveillance.

Still, it was a breach of trust. If they weren't being honest about that, what else were they lying about? What else were they hiding from me? What else did they spend so much time trying to get me to accept as the truth when it was anything but?

"Earth to Daddy," Macy said.

"Sorry, honey. I've just got a lot on my mind."

"It's Christhtmasth Eve," she said.

"Yes, it is." I stepped forward to hug her. I held her tight. So tight that I didn't notice what was about to happen.

24

I DON'T KNOW where he came from. I don't know how he made his move so quickly. It happened with far greater force and determination than when he'd managed to jam a paw into my crotch the day before.

He was an animal, driven by instincts that overcame whatever commands we'd somehow managed to get him to obey. And one thing we'd never been able to teach him to do was to not take full advantage of any opportunity to snarf any and all people food that made its way within the radius of a lunge, snatch, and escape.

While Linda breaded the fish and I hugged Macy, Buster sensed an opening. Swooping and leaping and corralling with his long, narrow snout. He got just enough of the mass protruding over the top of the pan to pull the entire thing from the edge of the stove and down to the floor.

Macy shrieked. Linda yelled. I stood there, dumbfounded, as Buster gnawed on the top of the chunk of slowly-cooked ham until it crashed to the tile. I pushed Macy away from the splash of still-scalding juices from the bottom of the pan.

I grabbed the dog. He locked his teeth into the top of the ham, which was now fully on the floor. I heard Linda rattling off a stream of swear-jar-worthy phrases as I clamped my bare hands onto the slab of the main course for our Christmas Day meal and engaged in an impromptu porcine tug-of-war that the canine was determined to win. I shouted over and over again—"Buster! No!"—until he ripped off a chunk and sprinted away with it.

I should have told Macy to let him go. I was more concerned about taking care of the rest of the mess. About scooping up the ham and putting it back in the pan and acting like it was no big deal. Like I'd salvaged it. Minus the piece with which Buster had absconded.

Linda continued to emit a chain of mostly PG-13 expletives as I tried to piece it all together. Macy, meanwhile, chased Buster out of the kitchen and into the family room. Just as I repositioned most of the ham and the pan onto the stove, I heard the crash.

He'd scurried behind the tree, growling and snarling and refusing to surrender the section of ham that Macy should have just let him keep. Whether it was Buster or Macy, one of them had snapped the fishing line. And down came the tree.

I slipped and slid on the hot wetness that had spilled out of the pan, trying to get to the next room to confirm what the sound had suggested. I could hear both Linda complaining and Macy crying when I first saw the tree, dark and flat with the bulb sticking up from the mouth of the steel tub. The wildebeests stampeded up the stairs at the ruckus. The cacophony grew and grew until I heard myself shouting.

"Everybody stop! Right now! Stop!"

Silence descended on the room, but for the noises coming

from Buster, who was cowered in the corner, still chewing on the Christmas ham he'd snatched from right under my nose. Macy's tears had become a muted sniveling, a reaction either to what had happened or my response to all of it. The boys stood there, taking it all in.

Linda emerged from the kitchen. "That damn dog," she said.

"It's not the dog's fault," I said. "The dog did what dogs do."

"Then it's your fault," she said. "Christmas dinner is ruined. And it's all your fault."

"He didn't get much of it. We can still eat the rest."

"I'm sure I'm going to serve that tomorrow," Linda said. "Funny story about the ham. The missing piece is from where the dog ripped it away with his mouth. *Bon appetit.*'"

"What am I supposed to do, Linda?"

"You can take him to the pound."

"No!" Macy said. "It'sth not Busthter's fault! Daddy sthaid stho!"

"Mommy doesn't mean that," I said to Macy. I turned to Linda. "Tell her you don't mean that."

Linda stormed out of the room. The boys were still standing there, watching it all.

"What are you two looking at?" I said, regretting my tone immediately.

"I told you it was gonna fall," Mark said.

I went to the garage, yanking the door open and turning on the lights. I scanned the area until I saw a leash. I grabbed it and returned.

"Don't take him to the pound!" Macy screamed. "Don't take Busthter away!"

"I'm not," I said to her. "I'm taking him for a walk. I need some air. Buster does, too. If he throws up, I'd rather him do it outside."

"Mommy!" Macy yelled. "Daddy's taking Busthter to the pound! Tell him not to do it!"

"Macy!" I said, much more loudly than I should have. "I told you I'm not taking him to the pound. I'm taking him for a walk. I need some air."

"Can I come, too?" she said, snivels re-escalating toward another full-blown meltdown. "Can I make sure you don't take Busthter to the pound?"

"Macy," Linda declared from the kitchen, in her front-of-classroom voice. "Your father isn't taking Buster to the pound. Let him go. You have to let him go."

There was something about the way she said the last sentence that made me wonder whether Linda would soon be having a very different conversation with Macy about letting Daddy go. I had a vision for an instant of a crappy one-bedroom apartment in which I'd be living alone, maybe by the middle of January.

I rushed toward Buster, who continued his wild-eyed chomping on the mostly-done ham. I jerked his collar, attached the leash, and yanked him away from the corner. I cranked the knob, swung the door open, led him out of the house. I didn't close it behind me.

As I exited, I caught a glimpse of the cat. He was once again perched on the couch, watching it all in the placid way he watched everything. Like he knew exactly what had happened. Like he knew that it was going to happen before it did. Like he also knew precisely what was going to happen next.

I didn't grab a coat. I regretted it not long after leaving the house. Though it wasn't sub-freezing, a sweatshirt and jeans weren't nearly enough to stay comfortable with the outdoor air in the upper thirties. Even with the extra layer or two of flesh I planned to start shedding after the holidays.

But, hey, at least I was still wearing my slippers. I dragged my feet through the first few steps to fully dry the bottoms, after the Christmas ham obstacle course.

Buster hurried to finish off the chunk of ham he'd wrested from the rest of it, fighting against the leash so he could chew and swallow, chew and swallow. Eventually, he realized we were taking a walk. He slipped into his half-prance, half-strut mode, seemingly anxious to see and be seen, even if there was no one to be seen or to do the seeing.

The homes in our development, a long oval of houses that connected to the main road that cut through this specific part of town, radiated with the season. Christmas lights of various colors and shapes adorned bushes and doorways and gutters and downspouts. It was quiet, calm. No one was coming or going. The asphalt loop lacked sidewalks or trees.

Buster usually watered the fire hydrant three doors down from our house. Consistent placement of his spray in the same spot over and over again had caused the paint to erode at his normal point of impact.

After Buster had finished, we kept going. I wasn't sure how long to stay away. I wished it was closer to midnight. Maybe I could have avoided going to church. Maybe I wouldn't go anyway. Maybe Linda wouldn't want me to.

She would, I knew. She'd already said we owed it to the kids. No matter what happened after that Christmas, she didn't want it to be, among other things, the year their father didn't accompany the family to mass. I sighed at the realization I'd have to sit there for more than an hour, listening to things I'd heard many times before.

How many times can you absorb the same readings, prayers, homilies? I wanted something to challenge me spiritually. Maybe the concept of organized religion worked better when the average human life lasted far less than seventy years. After a certain number of times hearing the same stories over and

over, there's no real reason to keep hearing them again and
again.

I was relieved Buster hadn't yet thrown up the ham. I realized I hadn't thrown up in more than a day. I wondered if,
later that night, I'd once again be visited by the Ghost of
Christmas Vomit.

I glanced up ahead. Someone was on the road, walking
along the other side of it. Coming my way. The movements
were familiar. The shape became recognizable. I looked
behind him for the Chevy as I heard him start to speak.

"Are you walking that dog or is that dog walking you?"

"A little of both," I said to the old man.

"Where's your coat?"

"I made a quick exit."

"So what happened? Did you spill something? Burn something? Did the dog tear something up?"

"Well, Buster here got a mouthful of tomorrow's ham," I
said, "and then he knocked down the tree."

"Dogs being dogs. That's why we never had one."

"I didn't have one growing up, either."

"That's what I just said."

"What did you say?" I asked.

"I said we never had one."

"Right. And I said I didn't have one, either."

"That's what I said."

"You said what?" I said.

"We never had one."

"I didn't, either."

"That's. What. I. Said."

"So you didn't have a dog or I didn't have a dog?"

"Exactly."

"Exactly what?" I said.

"We never had one."

I shook my head. I laughed. "I suppose you don't want this one?"

"We wouldn't be able to take him back with us."

"Back where?"

"Back home. I keep telling you, we're on our way home."

"I've seen you like ten different times in three days. You've said you're on your way home, over and over again. Why aren't you there by now?"

"Maybe we are."

"That makes no sense."

"Maybe it doesn't."

"Where's your car? Where's your wife?"

He pointed randomly behind his coat. "Back there. I ran out of gas."

"Where are you going?"

He dropped his chin and looked over his glasses at me.

"I mean where are you going right now?" I clarified.

"I was going to ask you to get us some gas. I don't have a can. Maybe you do? You can't say you're too busy to help this time. You're not going anywhere. You're not doing anything."

"You've got me on that one," I said. "Besides, Macy wouldn't be happy with me if I didn't help her two new favorite people. Come with me. I've got a can for the lawnmower. We'll put that in your tank. That'll be enough to get you to a station. There's one close by."

I turned back toward the house. I noticed Buster hadn't reacted to the old man at all. Not a bark or a sniff or anything. Maybe the ham wasn't agreeing with him, after all. We started walking, the old man, Buster, and me.

"How long have you lived here?" I asked.

"Lived where?"

"Here. In town."

"We don't live in town."

"So you drive in on Sundays?"

"Drive in for what?"

"For church," I said.

"Church? Oh, we haven't been to church in a long time."

"But my boys said they've seen you in church. You and your wife."

"Unless she's found herself another man as handsome as me, that wasn't us. Of course, if she does have someone else, I figure the last place they'd carry on is in church."

I stopped walking. I turned toward the man, faced him. I wasn't angry. But I was getting a little frustrated. I felt like he'd been toying with me, with all of us, from the instant I first saw him standing behind the trunk of his car on the shoulder of Route 32.

"Sir," I said, "exactly who are you?"

He smiled at me. "You still don't know, do you?"

"How would I know?"

"I think you do. I think you're afraid to admit it."

"Why would I be afraid to admit it?"

He gave a flimsy little shrug. "You know why."

"Why are you here?"

"You'll find out later," he said. "She'll explain it to you. I'd get it all twisted up."

"What's to explain?"

"Don't try to pry it out of me. She'll be upset with me. She wants to do it."

"When is this supposed to happen?"

"When it's supposed to happen."

I looked at him more carefully. "Do me a favor," I said.

He pulled out a wad of bills. "You finally want some of my money?"

"No," I said. "Take off your glasses."

He pulled the broad frames with the thick lenses away with

a shaky left hand. He began blinking through the cold air. I studied his face. I tried to peel back the years. Ten of them. Fifteen. Twenty.

"This isn't possible," I said.

"All things are possible," he replied.

He put his glasses back on. "You've got to be getting cold," he said.

I nodded, I turned. We started walking again, toward the house. My brain rumbled with thoughts. It was refusing to process what was happening. I finally thought of another question to ask, of the right words to use. I jerked my head around.

He was gone.

I spun my body, searching with my eyes along the asphalt for any sign of him, standing or walking or on the ground. Once again, he'd managed to vanish.

"I really do have a brain tumor," I said. Buster barked when I finished, and we continued making our way back to the house.

As we reached our driveway, I saw a small car. It came around the corner at the far end of the development. It slowed down and started up again. I could see things flying toward porches and doors. The Christmas morning paper, delivered much earlier than usual, news locked in place for a world that slowed to a standstill, if only for one day of the year.

The person driving the car delivered a paper to nearly every house, each one wrapped in a transparent blue plastic sleeve chucked in the general direction of its destination from the open windows on either side of the front seat.

I squinted as the car got closer to me. I saw a spoiler on the back end of it. The car stopped. I heard a voice. "You want your paper, mister?"

I stepped toward the car, put my hand on the spot where the window had slid into the door on the passenger's side. I squeezed. Metal on one side, plastic on the other. It was real, or at least it felt that way.

He handed me a newspaper, like the others tucked in the same blue bag. His arm was thin. His face was narrow. His mustache was ratty. He had a lightning bolt piercing above his eyebrow.

"Merry Christmas," I said to him.

He let go of the paper. He didn't say anything. He didn't react to me at all.

As he drove away, I saw the crack in the car's spoiler.

25

BUSTER AND I returned to a quiet house. The cat had
gone back to his spot on the shelf in the garage, as content
to be away from the dysfunction as he was to be smack dab in
the middle of it. The dog's labored breathing disrupted the
silence in the kitchen. I couldn't tell whether dinner had been
finished and eaten or entirely abandoned. I wasn't quite sure
how long I'd been gone.

My phone was on the island in the kitchen. I'd left so
quickly that I failed to realize I didn't have it with me. The
screen told me it was three minutes after nine o'clock. It
couldn't have been past six when I left. There's no way I'd
been gone for three hours.

A crash of nausea returned. I fought it off. The sheer panic
regarding the lost time must have given me special powers of
digestive-system control. I pondered for a second or two the
zany possibility of alien abduction.

I kept coming back to the concern, the conviction, that I

had a brain tumor. Probably malignant. Possibly metastasized. Potentially inoperable.

But someone would have seen me out there, wandering or whatever I'd been doing for three hours. I put a hand under Buster's snout and pulled his face toward mine. He seemed fine. Not traumatized or affected in any way by being in the elements for that long, or wherever we'd been.

I'd sometimes catch myself wondering what the dog and the cat were thinking. I would have written a very big check to secure access to Buster's actual thoughts in that exact moment.

Buster pulled his head away. His thick and complicated nose twitched. He probably could still catch a whiff of ham, hanging in the air. The ham. That stupid ham.

I removed his leash and tossed it in the garage, before heading for the TV room. The tree was upright again, and the lights glowed. I wandered behind it. New fishing line attached the trunk to the window. This time, they'd used two separate strands. I smiled.

I stood there, straining to hear anything. The cars were in the garage, so they were home. Unless they went to look for me on foot. I doubted they'd do that. The boys wouldn't have noticed I hadn't come back until morning, at the earliest. For Linda, at this point who knows when it would have registered? Only Macy would have been alarmed. The fact that she wasn't there to rush and greet me suggested she wasn't overly concerned, at least not yet.

I plotted my next move. I wasn't ready to deal with Linda. But I wanted to know where the kids were. The most likely location of the boys dawned on me. I could hear Macy's voice in my head, saying the name of the game.

Sthabotage.

I headed to the basement door and made my way down

the stairs. Our old flatscreen TV sat on a table that dated back to my law school apartment days. Attached to the set was the video-game console.

I constantly harped on them to keep it clean down there. They constantly ignored me. Empty water bottles and soda cans were scattered on the ground, a mess they'd already accumulated since Linda's Christmas party two nights earlier. Empty bags of chips, the little ones from the variety packs they both devoured on a non-stop basis, were strewn on every flat surface, including the pool table, crumbs on felt that was frayed in more than a few spots. I could see more of the small bags peeking out from the cushions on the couch across from the television.

The game had Joseph's full attention. Mark's face once again focused solely on his phone. They weren't startled when I spoke. They'd carefully mastered the art of being aware of their surroundings while also being entirely oblivious to them.

"Where's your mom?" I said. Neither answered.

"Boys, where's your mother?" They ignored me again, one apparently assuming the other would do the talking, and vice versa. Joseph sensed me swooping toward the power button on the monitor.

"She was on the phone earlier."

"The phone?" I said.

He glanced up at me for a second, without stopping any of the button-pressing and thumbstick-manipulating he was doing.

"Yeah. The phone. You know, you talk on it?"

"Who was she talking to?"

"Someone," Joseph said.

"Thank you for narrowing the field."

"Doing what now?"

"Never mind. Where's Macy?"

"She went to bed. She was upset. Mom told her to take a nap. So she won't fall asleep in church."

"She'll also be up all night," I said.

"It's Christmas," Joseph said, adroitly shrugging his shoulders and tilting his head while continuing to work the controller. "She'll be up all night anyway. You know how kids are."

"Yes," I said, staring down at him. "Indeed I do."

I glanced over at Mark, still lost in his screen. "What's Kelly Prater up to?" I said.

His face disengaged from the phone, eyes widening. "Did you see her somewhere?"

"Just making sure you're not catatonic, son."

"That was one of our vocabulary words last week," Joseph said, full focus otherwise on the game.

"I have a feeling you'll be learning plenty of new words soon," I said.

"We get ten more every week," he said, completely missing the point. Not realizing I was thinking of terms like *irreconcilable differences* and similar phrases that would become household fixtures if things were going to unfold after the holidays the way I sensed they would.

Then I thought of the brain tumor. Would she be less likely or more likely to kick me out if I have cancer? Or would it not change things? I tried to stop thinking about it.

I started singing *Silver Bells*. I added my twist on the second line from when I was a kid. They didn't react. Either they didn't hear what I'd said, or they didn't think it was funny. Regardless, it was like I wasn't even there.

Well, at least the adjustment won't be very difficult for them.

I climbed the stairs. I felt a little winded when I got to the top, a reminder that I needed to get my act together after the holidays. Maybe I'd join a gym. If I wasn't getting chemother-apy. I kept trying to push those thoughts away.

I wanted to go check on Macy. That would give me a way to let Linda know I was home without having to be the one to make the first move toward an interaction. Buster was in the kitchen, still rapid-fire sniffing for the ham that had been there. I wondered whether the rest of it had been dumped in the trash can. If it was, I couldn't smell it. Maybe that was another byproduct of the tumor.

Stop it, I told myself. *Just stop it.*

I kept walking through the kitchen and the TV room. I saw the tree again. I was impressed that the zombies who were parked in the basement had managed to get it fixed. Then again, they'd had three hours or so to do it.

Up the stairs I went, to the second floor. I walked softly. I didn't want to wake Macy before whenever Linda wanted her to get up. I still wanted to see Macy, even if she was sound asleep and stayed that way.

The hallway was dark, but not so empty of light that I couldn't see where I was going. I made my way to Macy's room. I knew how to properly twist the knob and open the door in a way that made no noise at all.

"Daddy?"

"I'm here," I whispered. "You're supposed to be asleep."

"I can't sthleep," she said quietly. "I was stho worried about you and Busthter. You didn't take Busthter to the pound, did you?"

"He's downstairs," I said. "He's fine."

"Then Sthanta heard me," she said.

"What do you mean?"

"I told Sthanta to keep my presentsth. I justht wanted Busthter back."

"Santa will still bring you presents."

She shot up in the bed. I pressed an index finger over my lips. "But I promisthed him. I promisthed Sthanta. If Busthter comes back, no presentsth."

"I talked to Santa. I told him Buster was fine, that he should still bring you presents."

"No you didn't."

"If you can talk to him, I can, too. He told me you offered to give up your presents if Buster came home. I told him Buster would be fine, that he didn't need to do anything about Buster."

I knew she bought it when she started giggling.

"Shhhhh. You're supposed to be sleeping. Try to sleep until Mommy wakes you up."

"I will. Thank you, Daddy. You sthaved Christhtmasth."

I thought about what she said. I smiled and stood there for a little while, watching the little body that fought to stay still. I turned and left, as quietly as I'd entered.

When I got back to the hallway, I saw that the door to our bedroom was open.

"She's supposed to be sleeping," I heard Linda say.

I walked in, already feeling like it was some sort of strange, foreign territory. "She is."

"I heard you two talking. You woke her up."

"She was awake," I said, keeping my voice low. "She was worried about the dog you wanted me to take to the pound."

"I said I didn't mean it."

"She didn't know that," I said.

"Where did you go?"

"I took the dog for a walk."

"For three hours?"

"I lost track of time."

"You didn't have a coat. Did you go to someone's house?"

"No," I said, not entirely sure whether I might have. I thought I didn't. I hoped I hadn't. That definitely would have supported the brain tumor theory.

"How were you gone that long?"

"I just was. It's not like you cared. It's not like you came and looked for me."

"So that's what this is about? You were testing me?"

"I'm not testing you. I don't need to test you. I already know all the answers."

"What's that supposed to mean, John?"

"Whatever you want it to mean."

"Why are you doing this on Christmas Eve?"

"I'm not doing anything. The dog did something that dogs sometimes do. You freaked out. Macy was afraid I really did take him to the pound. She told me she made a deal with Santa that if Buster came back she didn't want any presents."

"That's crazy."

"Well, she's five."

Linda trudged into the bathroom and said nothing more. It was the closest I'd ever get to a concession from her. "Are you going to church with us?" she said from the other side of the door.

I wanted to ask whether I had to, but I knew how it would go from there. She wanted me to go. Deep down, I suppose I wanted to go, if only to have one last normal event outside the home with the entire family, until whatever it was that was going to happen after the holidays.

It wouldn't take me long to get ready. I'd wear one of my work suits. I had plenty of clean shirts.

"We should leave by eleven," she called from the bathroom.

"Eleven? It starts at twelve."

"We won't get a good seat if we wait too long."

"I have a feeling we don't need to get there an hour early to get good seats. Besides, it's church, not a Bruce Springsteen concert."

"What does that mean?"

"What's there to see? Unless the live nativity scene is actually going to include a real birth, there won't be much drama."

"So you're saying you'd actually like to watch a live birth?"

"I'm saying nothing remotely that interesting will happen. Who cares where we sit?"

"Fine," she said. "We'll leave at five minutes until twelve. How's that?"

I wanted to say it was perfect. I knew better. "We'll leave at eleven," I said.

I left the room before she could respond. I was hungry. And I was curious about the whereabouts of the ham. I didn't want Buster to be the only one who'd gotten to enjoy an unauthorized chunk of it. If it was in the trash, I'd carve my way through the outer layer and give that part to the dog before helping myself to everything under it.

When I got to the kitchen, I couldn't believe my eyes.

26

THE OLD MAN was standing there. In the kitchen. By the refrigerator.

I almost didn't recognize him at first, since his hat wasn't covering his head. He held the fedora in front of him. He fiddled with the small red feather in the thick black band. His hair was white, coarse. He had a small bald spot near the rear of his scalp but his head was otherwise covered with closely-cropped bristles that pointed in every possible direction.

"How did you get in here?" I said.

"I tried to come down the chimney, but I couldn't figure out how to get to the roof."

I laughed at that. I waited for him to continue.

"The garage door was up," he soon said.

"I could have sworn I put it down."

"Well, the door would likely swear otherwise," he said.

"What happened to you out there?"

"Out where?"

"Outside. Remember? You needed gas?"

"I did?"

"You're not funny," I said to him.

"You're not exactly Henny Youngman, either."

"You have a habit of showing up quickly, and of disappearing even faster."

"I go where I'm allowed to go."

"Allowed? By who? Your wife?"

He looked at me and smiled. "No, not her. She thinks she's in charge. But she knows deep down she isn't. We go where we go. Where we can. When we can. Most of the time, we don't even decide. We're just there. Then, we're somewhere else."

He seemed confused, even a little scared. I didn't know what to say to any of it.

"Well," he said, "I don't know much. But I know that, for now, I wanted to tell you that we can't come to dinner tomorrow."

"Why not? Macy is really looking forward to it. I guess I am, too."

"We're on our way home," he said.

"You've been telling me that since Friday morning."

"And it's been true every time I said it. By tomorrow, we'll be home. So we can't be here. I wish we could."

"Where's your wife?"

"She's out in the car."

"Can I go tell her goodbye?"

Something flashed over his face. I couldn't tell what it was. "It's not time to tell her goodbye."

"But you're leaving?"

"Not yet. I just wanted you to know we won't be here for dinner. We've still got a little time."

I immediately felt thirsty, so much that I didn't think I could speak another word without some water. I raised a finger and turned to the cabinet for a glass. I filled it at the sink, took a long drink, turned back around.

Of course, he was gone.

I checked my phone. It was half past ten. I forced myself to accept that I'd been home from my three-hour walkabout for nearly ninety minutes, even though it felt like maybe thirty, at the absolute most.

I wondered for the first time whether the past three days had been a dream. Maybe a nightmare. Whatever it was, it didn't seem real. Maybe I'd wake up. Maybe this is what it always feels like when you're deep in the middle of a REM-sleep experience, and you just can't remember the sensation after it's over.

I had no choice but to embrace my current reality, unreal as it might have been. I decided to be helpful. I went to the basement stairs and yelled for the boys to go upstairs and get ready for church. They didn't answer. I yelled again. I sighed loudly and started down the steps.

When I got to the bottom, they weren't there. And so it was another climb, another reminder at the top that I had plenty of work to do to get myself in shape. Another migration through the main level of the house, and up the next set of stairs I started.

The second floor buzzed with activity. Nearly every light was on. The door to Joseph's room swung open. I stuck my head inside. The perpetual smell of dirty feet greeted me.

"When did you come up here?"

"I don't know. Whenever Mom texted us."

"Where was I?"

"You were in the kitchen. At the sink."

"What was I doing?"

"I don't know. Why are you asking me?"

"I just thought I'd notice you going by."

"You didn't act like you did. It looked like you were staring out the window."

I stopped right there. I didn't want to alarm him. Another question or two could make him start wondering whether something was wrong with me. Because, obviously, something was.

"We're leaving at eleven," I said.

"I know. Mom told us."

I nodded at him and went to our bedroom. Linda was back in the bathroom. I stepped into the closet and got dressed. I probably needed to shave, and I would have benefited from a fresh layer of deodorant. I opted for one of my industrial-strength, sweat-soaking T-shirts instead.

When I emerged from the bedroom, I heard Macy and her *pa-rum-pum-pum-pum*-ming, again. I hated to admit it had grown on me. I decided the sound of it would never, ever annoy me. She rumbled out of her room in a green dress that was maybe one size too big. A black belt cinched the material together.

She hugged me. "Merry Christhtmasth Eve," she said, face beaming and eyes dancing behind her glasses. I wanted that to never end.

"Is everyone ready?" Linda said from behind me, classroom voice projecting into Joseph's and Mark's rooms. They emerged on cue, and the family of five descended the stairs, one after the other. I wondered whether it was the last time it would happen exactly like that.

We made our way to Linda's SUV. Buster was still snuffling around in the kitchen. I couldn't remember if he'd been in there while I was talking to the old man. If I ever was talking to the old man.

Once in the garage, everyone took their seats for the full-family drive to church. Macy kept singing, "Pa-rum-pum-pum-pum."

Linda gently encouraged her to try something else. I didn't say anything.

Macy pivoted to *We Three Kings*. She knew some of the words, but not many of them. She settled on "star of wonder, star of night, star of royal beauty bright," repeating it on a loop that continued from the time the SUV backed out of the driveway until it pulled into the parking lot at the church. As Linda had predicted, it was already filling up.

"We should have come earlier," she said.

"We'll be fine," I replied. I turned off the engine, and the boys disengaged from their phones. "All devices stay in the car," I said to them. They both gave out a slight groan, but they complied more willingly than usual.

Macy led the way toward the side door we always entered and exited. Other families of various shapes and sizes headed the same way. The church was bathed in floodlights casting beams from the ground onto the stone, the stained-glass windows, the steeple. I looked around. Linda noticed me.

"Did you forget something?"

"No. Just looking to see if they're here."

"They who?"

"The old man and his wife. I think they go to church here."

"Why would you think that?"

I couldn't remember whether I had told her about breakfast, about the boys recognizing them from church. If I hadn't, I didn't feel like explaining it. "I just have a feeling they'll be here."

The pew where the family normally sat, typically without me, was empty. As soon as my rear end hit the seat, I remembered the hard and sturdy quality of the wood. It would be a long time sitting there until the ritual of standing, sitting, kneeling, lather, rinse, repeat would commence.

I took the spot at the end of the row, my right elbow slightly invading the aisle that led to the altar. Macy sat nestled between Linda and me, with Joseph to Linda's left and Mark next to Joseph.

Mark was looking around, probably trying to catch a glimpse of Kelly Prater.

With thirty minutes to go until midnight, the organ began to play a medley of religious carols. A choir of fifteen faithful, their ages spanning the decades, led the singing. I watched Macy the entire time. She tried to follow along in one of the booklets that had been handed to us on our way in. She could read maybe a dozen words, but she was determined to try to keep up with the print. From time to time, I pointed out the right place to her.

She had a quiet energy that sustained me through the next twenty minutes or so, as the church became more and more full. I studied the faces and the body language, trying to guess which ones were regulars and which ones showed up only on Christmas and Easter. The every-weekenders had an edge of quiet self-righteousness along with a hint of frustration that the twice-per-year interlopers were making the experience less comfortable and spacious than it usually was.

The choir stopped singing. The organist continued to play through portions of the various carols, moving from some the choir had sung to others that hadn't made their way to the official roster of songs. The lights stayed dim. The movement of bodies into the remaining seats provided a loose and random percussion. I felt myself relaxing, serenity descending upon me.

I became aware of my breathing, even and slow. My concerns were beginning to slip away. I allowed them to go. I relished the feeling. I could sense my entire body loosen. It was an unexpected but entirely welcome development.

I should have known it wouldn't last.

27

I FELT A hand tapping on my shoulder. It wasn't really tapping. It was the entire palm and fingers, slapping repeatedly against the edge of my clavicle.

I turned my head to the right.

"You got room for us in there?" The old man had his hat off again, but he was still wearing the rest of his usual ensemble, wrapped in the same overcoat that hung from him like a cape. His wife stood behind him and to the right.

"Hi!" Macy cried, far louder than she should have. A wave of soft laughter rolled through the congregation. She instantly seemed self-conscious. I began to tell her it was OK, but the presence of her new friends made her forget about it.

"Sit nextht by me," she squealed at them, struggling to control her volume. "Sit nextht by me."

Everyone slid to the left, and I switched places with Macy. She plopped herself between the old man, who settled into a spot next to me, and his wife, who had taken the place where

I usually sat, right on the edge of the pew. I didn't mind giving it up, especially since (if the old man truly had visited me in the kitchen earlier that evening) it was the last time we'd see them, at least for a while. Possibly ever.

I felt Linda tugging at the sleeve of my jacket. "Those are the Alexanders. They've been going to church here for years."

"So you see them?" I whispered.

"Excuse me?"

"I mean, that's who the boys said they were. We had breakfast with them. At Denny's."

"That's who they are."

"Macy said she'd never see them before."

"She's seen them pretty much every Sunday for pretty much all of her life."

I didn't respond to that. I tried not to think about it, either.

Macy and the old man's wife chattered in hushed voices. I listened, but I couldn't make out much of what they were saying to each other. Macy was happy, in its most pure and innocent form. I felt that wave of relaxation returning as the various bodies became settled in their chosen locations and waited for mass to begin.

It started promptly at midnight, with the same pomp and circumstance that it did every year. As if Jesus were tunneling his way out that very night. Maybe he was. I don't know. Something happens at times like those where all reason and sense become suspended, at least for a little while.

I fully participated in the service, to my own astonishment. Uttering the various responses and prayers in a loud, clear voice. Like I'd done when I was a kid, at mass with my parents and my brother. With genuine enthusiasm.

I could tell Linda was confused by whatever it was that had come over me. I knew it was temporary, but I didn't care. I was there. I might as well make the most of it. I even sang the various songs, my inability to carry a tune lifted and blended by the other voices operating mostly in unison.

We stood, we sat, we stood, we sat, we kneeled. The old man and his wife moved at a careful, tentative pace. I heard their joints creaking as they did. But they took part in each of the various movements and rituals that morph into second nature through years and years of repetition.

Maybe they really are the Alexanders, I thought. They seemed to be familiar with the church, comfortable in the surroundings. They shuffled along with everyone else for the procession that resulted in the distribution of communion.

Macy insisted on going, even though she was too young to receive the Eucharist. The priest made a sign of the cross on Macy's forehead. She told him in a loud and clear voice, "Thank you, Merry Christhtmasth."

The service ended with the priest and the altar servers processing back down the aisle as the entire church sang *Joy to the World.*

Joy. I was feeling something dangerously close to it.

After they passed, the song continued. When it ended, the old man and his wife began to exit the same way they came. Macy went with them. I followed, and the rest of the family created a line behind me.

We usually didn't leave through the front of the church. We passed the baptismal font, which when not being used for that purpose was filled with Holy Water.

Macy blessed herself with a little too much of it. I put my hand in as well, for the first time in a very long time. The water was cool but not cold. I pressed the wetness against my forehead before finishing the four-pointed gesture I'd first learned when I was Macy's age, forty years earlier.

We exited into air that carried a much more noticeable chill. The live nativity scene was arranged to the right. Macy

led the old man and his wife over to see it. I heard her saying she wanted to see *Baby Jesusth,* even though the part was
being played, as it always was, by a doll.

The rest of the cast wore the usual garb. They were standing and kneeling in their spaces, frozen in place while church-
goers gawked at a scene that was utterly devoid of any action.

The man playing the role of Joseph wore a large thick
beard that was obviously fake. It was too big for his face. It
looked borderline cartoonish.

Something beyond the brown-black fur caught my eye. He
had a piercing above an eyebrow. I could just make out the
shape of a lightning bolt.

He looked at me. Our eyes locked.

I smiled at him. He didn't smile back.

The crowd dissipated, in time. The old man and his wife
were there, and then they weren't. I had stopped being surprised by the speed with which they made their exits.

Linda said she was getting cold. I was, too. We worked our
way around the church to the SUV. Everyone piled in, once
again assuming their regular spots. We momentarily sunk into
the quiet, even Macy.

"That was nice," I said.

"Yesth it was," Macy said.

The boys already had their faces back in their phones.
Linda smiled. I didn't bother to figure out whether it was real.

During the drive home, Linda reminded the kids in a calm
but stern voice that it was straight to bed for all of them. None
resisted. They knew the drill on Christmas Eve, and they were
fine with it.

I pulled into the garage. Everyone filed out of the SUV
without conversation or much sound at all. Macy seemed
giddy, but she was content to go along with the next step
toward Christmas morning. Go to bed, try to sleep, at some

point fall asleep, wake up before everyone else, and work on jostling the rest of the family into consciousness so that the annual ritual of ripping a layer of wrapping from packages could begin.

The cat was back in his spot on the garage shelf, taking it all in without seeming to care. Or maybe silently passing judgment on the stupid, predictable things we were doing.

Buster greeted us, tail wagging and nose sniffing but otherwise content to receive a smattering of attention from Macy and the boys before the night settled into nothing. The kids removed their coats and shoes and headed for their rooms. I knew the boys would be messing with their phones into the wee hours, and that was fine. Once they were in their beds, they were officially out of my jurisdiction.

Linda went upstairs to change. I found the bottle of wine I'd opened that afternoon, not long before Buster had launched his assault on the ham. I poured a glass and sipped, waiting for Linda to return so that we could make the final preparations for morning.

I wondered if the old man would show up again, out of nowhere. I found myself expecting it.

He didn't. I didn't know whether I was relieved or disappointed.

As the first glass of wine emptied, I heard Linda coming down the steps. "Don't drink too much of that," she said. "I need your help with a few things."

"I'm at your disposal for whatever you need," I said, before refilling the glass. "Do you want some?"

"No, thanks."

"You always have a glass or two while we do this."

"My stomach's bothering me. And I'm tired. It'll knock me out."

"Where is everything?"

"In the basement. In the storage room. Where I always keep it. It's all ready. I just need you to bring it up. Macy's bike still needs to be put together. You said you'd do it."

"I did, and I will. It can't be that hard."

"The box is in the garage. The boys helped me put it under the workbench. It's heavy."

I put the glass down and flexed my muscles. "Not for me," I said.

She didn't laugh. My pose instantly flattened.

"You used to like that one," I said.

"I used to like a lot of things."

"Well," I said, taking another drink, "I still like a little wine. I hope that never changes."

"You should get started on the bike before you forget how to use a screwdriver."

"Who says I ever knew?"

Again, no laughter.

I went to the garage. When I flipped the light on, the cat's head spun toward me. He had a smug, knowing gaze.

"Screw you," I said to the cat. He seemed to be pleased he'd gotten me to react that way on Christmas Eve, especially since I didn't say "screw."

He kept staring at me, almost daring me to do something about it. I looked on the workbench for something I could throw at him. I didn't want to hurt him; I just wanted that expression to go away. But everything I saw could have actually injured the cat or ricocheted back into the Subaru, denting the metal or maybe even busting a window.

I turned from the cat, looking for the box containing the bike, tucked under a green garbage bag Linda had used to conceal it. I pulled a corner out from under the workbench and wedged it past the front end of the Subaru and along the grill of the SUV. I pulled the box up into the kitchen.

I looked up at the cat. He was still leering at me. I gave him the finger.

"Are you planning to drag that to the TV room?" Linda said.

"It's just cardboard."

"It can still mess up the wood."

"Unless there's a nail sticking out from the bottom of the box, it won't mess up the wood."

"Why don't you just carry it?"

I stopped, allowing the box to rock into place on the kitchen floor. "I can just open it and put it together here."

"You could have done that in the garage."

"It's a little cramped out there. Besides, this is the only quiet time we have between Christmas Eve and Christmas Day."

"Once you bring the presents up from the basement, I'm going to bed."

I muttered a curse word when I realized I'd forgotten about the stuff in the basement. I huffed and sighed and trudged down the stairs. I brought up as many packages as I could carry. Linda had wrapped each one of them with immaculate precision and tucked them away from any curious eyes.

Linda waited for me at the top of the stairs, taking some of the items from my hands and letting me put others on the floor before I went back for more. Our hands never actually made contact during the process. I couldn't tell whether she was deliberately trying to avoid it.

After four trips, I had moved everything to the first floor. I could feel a trickle of sweat on each side of my face. I tried to conceal that I was on the verge of gasping for breath. It didn't work.

"You need to get in shape," she said.

"I know. Starting right after the holidays."

"It's always right after something. For it to work, it needs to be right now."

"So you want me to go to the gym tonight?"

"No," she said, rolling her eyes. "Never mind. Enjoy the holiday. We'll turn over a new leaf on Tuesday."

"That's what I'm worried about," I muttered.

"What's that?"

"Nothing. Can you toss me a knife so that I can open this box?"

She pulled out the drawer containing the utensils and lifted a steak knife, with a black plastic handle and a serrated blade. She flipped it end over end. On any other night, I would have recoiled and let it hit the ground. That night, I snatched it from the air. I felt the sharp metal teeth dig into the flesh of one of my fingers, breaking through the skin in at least three places. I had no idea why I did it. I still don't know what made me catch the knife that way. I suppose I felt the need to prove that I was something other than whatever she considered me to be.

My focus shifted to assessing the damage, deciding whether I needed a couple of Band-Aids or risk smearing blood on Macy's new bike. The ragged tears in the prints of my fingers bled a little, but not enough to make me think it would be a problem.

I realized Linda was staring at me. "You're acting very strange."

"I'm not acting."

She shook her head and started for the steps. Before she left the kitchen, she stopped and turned back to me. "What got into you at church tonight?"

"What do you mean?"

"You don't go nearly as much as you used to, and there's no way you would have gone tonight if it wasn't a family activity. But you were acting like you were, I don't know, into it."

"I was."

"Then why don't you go more often?"

"I didn't plan to do that. It just happened."

"Why did it happen?"

"I don't know."

"Does it mean you'll start going to church again?"

"I don't know."

"Don't you see how odd that is? To show up and throw your-self into it but then not want to go back?"

"I hadn't thought about it. I don't get as much out of it as I used to. Maybe the right balance for me is to go sometimes. I know all of the readings. I know all of the stories. I know how they start. I know how they end."

"It's not about your entertainment."

"What is it about? Is God taking roll? Is there a magic num-ber of masses you have to attend in a lifetime? Or is it based on a percentage?"

"You should want to go."

"But why should I want to go? I used to think it was good for my law practice. Trust me, that's one of the reasons I went. But then I realized people aren't going to hire a lawyer based on the fact that they see his face in church every week. Hell, most people want a lawyer who doesn't know how to turn the other cheek or love thy neighbor. They want an asshole."

"That would be a great TV commercial for you," she said, "if you ever decide to make one. I'm John Persepio. Asshole At Law. It's actually kind of catchy."

"It's not funny."

"It's also not wrong. I've lived with you long enough to know the truth." She started to walk away.

"Yes," I said, "the truth is that I am an asshole. I know it. And I know that doesn't make it better. I also know I do the abso-lute best I can, every day, to provide for this family. Sometimes I feel like it's never enough. I try to make you proud of me, and I feel like it's never enough. If I did commercials and represented the family of every poor bastard who was ever splattered by a truck within a sixty-mile radius of here, I feel like it wouldn't be enough. There would be something else. There's always something else. You're always trying to hold me to a standard that, no matter what I do, I can't meet."

She turned just enough so that I could see her mouth move as she spoke. "I'm just trying to get you to push yourself to be more than you are."

"Why are you doing that?"

She spun a little more. "Because before your mother died she told me you needed that. She asked me to do it."

I stopped myself from falling down. "What did you say to her?"

"What do you think I said, John? I told her I would."

"Why didn't you ever tell me this before? In all these years?"

She turned and continued toward the steps. "Why didn't you ever ask?" she said, and then she climbed the stairs to the bedroom.

After she left, I forced myself to focus on the contents of the box. I removed the pieces with slow, deliberate movements, trying hard not to clang metal against metal. I arranged them on the floor in the kitchen. I placed them down with care, still hoping to make as little noise as possible. The hollow metal tubes made soft *tinks* when they landed against the tile floor.

As the last piece found its place among the various other parts of the bike on the ground in front of me, I stood up. I stopped. I listened.

There was another sound.

Someone was knocking on the front door.

28

I KEPT LISTENING. I didn't move. I could feel thumping in my neck, getting faster.

The sound stopped. Just as I began to tell myself it was nothing, it started again. A soft rapping, a tapping. I hustled over to the door before Linda could hear any of it. If she even could hear any of it. I didn't stop to think whether she actually could. I probably would have known the answer.

I also knew who was on the other side of the door before pulling it open. The knob turned, the door swung inside. And there they were.

The old man and his wife. Peering up at me. Smiling. The old man's glasses were foggy. I couldn't see his eyes through the lenses.

"Well, don't just stand there," he said. "Invite us inside."

"Butch," his wife said. "Don't be rude."

"I'm not being rude. It's cold out here."

"Come in," I said, pulling the door wider. "Please. Come in."

I stepped back, glancing up the stairs for any sign Linda had heard enough to pique her curiosity. They came inside, moving in the rickety way they always did. Slow and steady. Joints crackling as they stepped into the TV room and marveled at the tree.

"All is calm," the old man said, "all is bright."

"Just like every year," I replied. "The magic of Christmas Eve."

He stopped and turned toward me, glasses still misty on the inside. "Magic," he said. "Yes. Magic. Or something."

"You sound like you've been drinking," his wife said.

"I haven't had a drink in a long, long time," he said as he made his way toward the same spot where he'd sat and eaten— or sat and not eaten—a plate of food only two nights earlier. He dropped himself into the couch, not waiting for his wife to sit first.

"Do you want some wine?" I said.

"He doesn't drink anymore," she told me.

"I don't drink anymore because I never have the chance. Now, I have the chance."

"I'm not sure I want to be around you after your first glass of wine in twenty-two years," she said.

"You haven't had anything to drink in twenty-two years?" I said.

He paused, tilted his head. "I guess it has been twenty-two years. After a while, it all starts to blend together."

"What starts to blend together?" I asked.

He turned up his palms and shrugged. "This. Everything. Our current state of existence. Is it purgatory? Is it limbo? I don't know. All I know is we've been wandering for a long time. And now, after all this time, we end up wandering your way."

I looked at the woman. She was studying my reaction with a slight smile on her face. "You still don't know who we are, do you?" she said.

"I think I do. I thought I did. You're the Alexanders. From church."

She shook her head. "We're not the Alexanders, dear."

"But the kids recognized you. Linda recognized you."

"They saw what they needed to see," the woman said. "You saw the truth. Your little girl saw it, too."

"Why her?" I said.

"Why her?" she said. "Why you? Why anything? There's plenty of *why* in your world. We haven't been part of this world for a very long time, and we still don't know the answer to most of the *why*."

I turned my attention to the old man. I wanted to hear it from him. "So who are you?" I said.

"I always said you were smart," he said. "Maybe I was wrong."

"You never said he was smart," she said. "I said he was smart."

"No, I said he was smart when he learned to tie his shoes. I showed him one time and he had it. One time."

"I said he was smart when he memorized the multiplication tables. He was only seven. I made flash cards. Do you remember the one that always tripped you up?"

At first I didn't realize what she expected from me. And then the words fell over my lips.

"Eight times six is forty-eight," I whispered. "Eight times six is forty-eight."

"See," she said, turning to the old man. "He was smart then, and he's smart now."

I stumbled backward and began to fall. I caught myself. "Wait a minute," I said. "You're not."

The old man nodded and grinned. "We are."

"You can't."

"We can," his wife said. "We don't know why we can, but we can."

"Where did you come from?" I said.

"I still can't believe no one ever told you about the birds and the bees."

"No. I mean where did you come from now? You've been gone. For so long."

"Dear," my mother said, "we don't understand it much better than you do. We can't control it. We're just here. We don't quite know how we got here, the same way you don't quite know how you got here."

"*I* was told about the birds and the bees," my father interjected.

"Not that way," she said, her gentle voice patient and her dancing eyes probing mine for any hint of acceptance. "We died. We know we died. And now we're here. No one told us we were coming here. But here we are. And we know the years have gone by. It's just something we know."

"What else do you know?" I said.

"I know I really could use that glass of wine," my father said.

"We know our window is closing," she said. "We know we're leaving soon."

"You're on your way home," I said.

"Yes," she said, smile getting broader. "Although we're not quite sure what that means."

"Did you show up here so that you could say goodbye to me?"

My father looked away as I asked the question. My mother continued to stare at me. I noticed her eyes becoming wet.

"No," she said.

"They why are you here?"

She looked down at her lap before she continued. "We want you to come with us."

That was when I fell, right onto my ass. My arm crashed into the collection of cast-iron tools for a fireplace we rarely used. The poker fell toward my face. I caught it just before the long thick bar flattened my nose. I held it there and listened for Linda. I had little desire to explain to her that the elderly couple from church who were actually my long-deceased parents had decided to show up out of the blue and harvest their first-born son for a permanent trip to the great beyond.

I worked my way back to my feet. "Come with you?" I whispered to them, in a quiet but sharp voice. "How would I come with you?"

"You just would," the old man said, seeming to lose interest in the back and forth. "It would just happen."

"Where would we go?" I asked, head turning back and forth as I spoke the words to both of them.

"Home," my mother said, as her right hand clasped my wrist. "We're going home."

"Where is home?"

"Anywhere," the old man said. "Everywhere. We haven't seen it yet, but we know. It's all around. People think heaven is up there. It's right here. It's just a different plane, or something. And we've been ending up on this side of it."

"But why?" I asked him.

"We don't know why," the woman said. "But we know this is what we are. Who we are. How far apart did we die?"

My eyes continued to shift and slide back and forth, taking in both of them as I did the math. "It wasn't very long," I said. "Eight months."

"Seven months, three weeks, two days, nine hours," she said. "I know how long it was, I felt every second of it. But also it went by in the blink of an eye. There was no delay, but there also was one. Then, just as we were still figuring out what was going on, we were here. In these bodies. The old people we would have become if we hadn't died, apparently."

"So now you're here for me?"

"That's what we think," she said. "I came for your father. After I died."

"So you two have just died?"

"Yes and no," she said. "It's been twenty-two years, but for us it really hasn't been. Besides, there's no rule book. It just is how it is. And we're still figuring it all out."

"I'm confused. Are you telling me that I'm dying? That this is what I see when I die? My parents coming to get me?"

"I suppose that's right, in a sense," she said.

"That's not all of it," my father said.

"What do you mean?" I said.

"Well, you have a choice," he said. "You can come home with us, or you can stay."

"That seems way too simple."

"Simple is better than the alternative," my mother said. "Simple is a gift. You having this choice is a gift. Not everyone gets it."

"Did you?" I said to my father. "Could you have chosen to stay?"

He turned away from me. "I missed my wife. I'm sorry. There was nothing else for me."

"You had me," I said. "You had your sons."

"I didn't want her to be alone. It wasn't an easy decision, but in the end it was."

"You now have a decision to make," my mother said.

"Can I sleep on it? For a night or two?"

"We need to know now," she said. "We're on our way home now."

"None of this makes any sense."

"Join the club," my father said. "Remember, we're just figuring it out, too. Basically."

"Why are you saying 'basically'?" I said. "I feel like there's more to this."

My mother looked at my father. "I told you he was smart," she said.

"Not like the other one."

"What about the other one?" I said.

"Never mind the other one," my father said. "He's still not sure what he wants. Not that it matters."

"You're not referring to Michael," I said.

"I'm not referring to anyone. I'm referring to you. You have to decide. Are you going home with us, or aren't you?"

"I can't," I said. "I have a family."

"We're your family."

"I have people who rely on me."

"Do they?" my father said.

"Butch."

"He knows what he's been thinking. He knows what he's facing."

"Stop," she said, in a loud voice that made me flinch. It was loud enough for Linda to hear it, if Linda could actually hear it.

"What am I facing?" I said.

"You know what you're facing," my father said. "You don't need me to spell it out."

"So what will happen to Linda, to my kids? I jump to when they die, and it all continues until the line fizzles out? This makes no sense, at all."

"I don't know," my mother said. "All I know is that we're going home, and that you have a chance to join us. I have no idea how it will work for Linda or for anyone else in your family."

"What if I don't go?"

"You keep living," my father said. "But it's not going to be easy. I think that's why you're getting this chance. Not everyone gets this chance."

"How do you know that?"

"I just do. I can't explain it any better than that."

I stood there, processing all of it. Trying to understand it. Knowing I never would or could. I had a decision to make. On the surface, it was easy. I'd stay. I would definitely stay.

But then I started to think about it. They knew about Linda. Did they know whether I have a brain tumor? Why stick around for a bunch of misery and illness? Why have my family remember me as a shell of who I was? Why not just go now? They'd have the life insurance money. Linda would find someone else. She was going to anyway. At least she technically wouldn't be committing adultery.

Then it hit me. What would a choice to go count as? They were giving me an offer to leave. It's not really suicide. It's a path away from whatever it was I was going to be dealing with. I wasn't doing anything to myself. I was just going with them.

"What happens if I go?" I said. "What happens to, you know, my body?"

They looked at each other. Neither wanted to speak.

"It would look like you had a heart attack," my mother said. "You'd fall on the ground. That would be that."

"On Christmas morning? That's not acceptable. That would ruin Christmas for my children for the rest of their lives."

"Couldn't we make it happen the day after?" my father said to my mother.

"Butch, don't say those things."

"But it's true," my father said to my mother. "You know it's true." He turned toward me. "We may have some leeway here. We'd come back Tuesday. You'd still have Christmas with your family. And your family wouldn't have to find you on Christmas morning."

"This is incredibly confusing," I said.

"It is and it isn't," she said. "It's no more confusing than anything else about living."

"When do I need to make a decision?"

"Soon," my father said.

"And once I make it, I can't change my mind?"

"It's binding," he said. "Final and binding."

"That doesn't make any sense."

"Does any of this make any sense?" he said. "It makes no sense to me, and I'm far closer to it than you."

"So I just have to tell you whether I'm going or not? Right now?"

My mother looked at my father. Then she looked back at me. "Well," she said, "not right now. You might want to talk to someone else first."

"Linda?" I said.

"Not her," my mother said. "Someone else. He should be here soon."

Before I could ask the question, I knew the answer. Before I could tell them I knew the answer, I heard more knocking on the door.

This time, it was hard and persistent and impatient.

29

I RUSHED TO the door, still concerned that someone upstairs could hear the racket, even if I knew they couldn't. I yanked the knob and pulled the edge of the wooden panel past my face.

The first thing I saw was the lightning bolt above his eyebrow, catching a gleam from the light inside the house. Then the gaunt face, cheekbones slicing through the steam wafting from his mouth and nose, ratty mustache slipped between the two.

It was him. It was Michael. Baby Michael.

Fifteen years after his own demise. Self-inflicted. I was the one who'd found him. Eyes bulging. Mouth open. Tongue protruding. Like the faces we'd make to each other at the dinner table when our parents weren't watching. That's when I remembered I'd made myself forget what he looked like.

I displayed no pictures of him. I was angry he'd done it.

And he knew it. I realized that's why he'd been so standoffish, everywhere I'd seen him.

"Well," he said. "I'm here. They told me to be here. Now what?"

"Do you want to come in?" I said.

"No."

"Why not?"

"Because you don't want me in your house."

"Why do you say that?"

"You've erased me from your entire life. I know you have. It's like I never even existed. You've never told your kids anything about me, not once."

I didn't try to argue with him. I knew it was true. The next sentence flew from my mouth before I could try to stop it. "I'm not the one who killed myself," I said.

"You're an asshole."

"I thought ghosts would be nicer."

"We all ain't Casper."

I didn't respond for several seconds. "You never really liked that one," I said.

"Huh?"

"Casper. I liked Casper cartoons. You didn't."

"Happy little dead kid," he said. "I never thought the dead were happy. Now I know they're not."

"Come inside," I said. "They're here."

"I know they're here. They've been driving me crazy. I like that they're focused on you for a change. I needed a break from them."

I looked over my shoulder. They were sitting on the couch but not really paying attention to us. Almost as if they were letting us do what they knew we needed to do. I stepped outside and pulled the door shut behind me. "Did they come get you, too?"

"Yes and no. I was already gone. They didn't give me a choice like the one they're giving you."

"Why am I getting a choice?"

My brother shrugged. "I don't know. I don't know what's going on. Is this heaven? Hell? Somewhere in between? I never believed in any of that stuff. Now I'm living in it."

"Or not living in it."

He tilted his head and narrowed his right eye, apparently not sure how to take that. Then I heard something I hadn't heard my brother do in years.

He laughed. He laughed like he always had, from the time he was old enough to make the sound while rolling around in a diaper full of his own poop. It was him. I wanted to hug him, but I wasn't sure how he'd take that.

"So what are you gonna do?" he said to me.

"I don't know. I thought I did. Now I don't. There's something to be said for walking away on your own terms."

"Except when I did it," he said.

"That's not what I mean. They're giving me a way out that isn't really a way out. Did you know that? They said it'll look like I had a heart attack."

"I had a feeling that's what they were up to. They haven't told me much. I don't know how much they've told you, but from our perspective we didn't die very long ago. Even though we're also aware of all the time that has passed. I can't describe it. We're existing in time and not in time, at the same time. I know I've been gone for fifteen years, but it doesn't feel like fifteen years have passed, in the same way you've experienced the past fifteen years."

"That's what I can't figure out. If I go, will it not feel like I had to wait decades to see my kids again?"

"You'll still see them. You'll still be around. But the time doesn't pass the same way. I can't really explain it. Remember when she was pregnant? You'd talk to me. I'd hear your voice. But I had no idea what was on the outside. I had no idea what it meant to exist beyond the womb."

"You remember that? Why did you never tell me?"

"I didn't remember it until after I died." He peered over my shoulder to confirm the door was closed. "I don't know what I'm allowed to tell you about this. But I can access everything I ever experienced. All the way back to before I was born. I can do it right now, while we're talking. I know it doesn't make sense to you. It eventually will, if you decide to go."

I found myself becoming more and more fascinated by the possibility of joining them. Of entering this new phase of being. The intrigue made me feel guilty. I'd be abandoning my family. But would they be better off without whatever was coming? Would it be better for the kids to have me gone all at once, or to see their parents split up and watch me fight a losing battle with whatever was growing inside my skull?

"Don't presume you'll die from whatever you have," he said. It felt like he was reading my mind.

"What do you mean?" I said, hoping to draw more from him.

"You're not destined to die in a few years, to wither away, to put your kids through that. Besides, they'd probably prefer that to not having you around at all."

"It sure would be nice if I could ask them."

"I don't know much about what's going on," he said, "but I know you can't do that. You've got to make this decision on your own. Not that anyone in your life would believe any of this, if you told them."

"I know I don't believe any of it."

"Well," he said, "you need to."

I was beginning to feel cold. I crossed my arms to get a little warmer. "Did they tell you I have to decide right now, but they'll wait until after Christmas to take me?"

"I heard them talking about that. She wants you to come. He's acting like he doesn't, but he does. I don't know how they managed to finagle this thing where you decide now and they come back later. I don't know who else they're talking to."

"There are others?"

"Others? There's everyone. Everyone who ever lived."

"Who's in charge?"

"I don't know," my brother said. "I haven't met him. Or her. Or whoever. I don't know if I'm in trouble or anything because I did it to myself. I feel like I only know what I need to know. But they definitely seem to know more than me. Maybe going to church every Sunday for their entire lives paid off."

I turned my head to the sky. I saw a few stars peeking through the clouds.

"It's not up there," he said. "There's no up or down. It's all around. Just like when I was inside her stomach and you weren't. But you're on the inside this time. And I'm on the outside."

"So is all that stuff they told us true?"

"Yes and no, as far as I can tell. There's something. But it's nothing anyone who is still alive can understand. So people just do the best they can. They're sort of on the right track, but you can't begin to comprehend any of it until after it happens. Even now, I don't know everything there is to know. I feel like I haven't even started to scratch the surface."

"They keep telling me they're on their way home. Do you know what that means?"

"They've been telling me the same thing since I died. And, no, I have no idea what it means."

"Is it a good thing or a bad thing?"

He stared at me for a long time, not saying a word. I felt the cold go away, like there was a fire in a stove that was gradually warming everything around me. "Here's the question I keep asking myself," he said. "Is it ever a bad thing to be going home?"

I nodded at that one. I felt my decision bubbling in that visceral well from which all big choices come. "Let's go inside and talk to them a little more," I said.

"You're sure you want me in your house?"

"Michael," I said, "I'm sorry for ever doing or saying or even thinking anything that would make you believe I didn't want you in my home."

For the first time since I'd seen him in all those different places, in all those different costumes and disguises, I finally saw him smile. As he did, he shifted into the man I remembered, the man I'd tried to forget. The one I'd seen the day before he died, the one who was in the basement watching football with me and drinking more beer than we should have that afternoon, laughing and enjoying the togetherness, same as always. I'd forgotten that feeling. I wanted more of it.

I turned to open the door. The knob wouldn't move.

"You have to make your decision now," he said. "Make it now. You don't have to go in and tell them. They'll know."

I tried the door again, while also trying to ignore the feeling that was hardening into resolution, deep inside me. Still nothing.

"I think I locked us out," I said. I shook my head and turned back to him. "It's just like the time—"

Michael was gone.

I got cold again. I knew my parents were gone, too. I could feel it. I closed my eyes, hoping that when I opened them I'd be inside the house. It felt colder and colder as I stood there. I tried to ignore it, pressing my eyes shut hard and praying I wouldn't actually be locked out of my own house on Christmas Eve.

I opened my eyes. The door was still in front of me, and I was still on the wrong side of it.

I didn't spend as much time as I should have coming up with an explanation before I started ringing the bell.

30

FEET RUMBLED DOWN the stairs, more than one set of them. They stopped. I could hear Linda giving directions. Her voice was muffled.

"Stay upstairs," probably. Authority oozing from her class-is-in-session voice. Then I could hear footsteps again, at a much slower pace.

"It's me," I said, nearly yelling the words. "I locked myself out."

"John?"

"Yes, it's me."

"How do I know it's you?"

I never knew why we didn't have a peephole in the front door. And I was the one who thought having security cameras on the house reeked of paranoia, especially in a small town where nothing interesting ever happened.

Nothing interesting, indeed.

"Am I inside the house? If I'm not inside the house, I'm out here."

She opened the door, hair pulled back and irritation radiating in my direction. "What are you doing out here?"

"I locked myself out."

"How did you lock yourself out?"

"Well, the door was locked and it closed behind me." As the words came out of my mouth, I wondered how I'd ever managed to win a single trial.

"Well, I realize that," she said, still glaring at me as I walked inside, rubbing my arms through a wave of shivers. "How did you end up outside with the door closed?"

I stopped moving. I was hoping to come up with something bordering on the semi-plausible. "I thought I heard something," I said, bobbing my head in the recognition that my explanation literally counted as landing in the loose vicinity of the truth.

"What did you hear?"

"Something," I said. "That's why I checked."

She followed me into the kitchen, hawk tracking a wounded squirrel. "But what was it?"

"I don't know," I said, continuing toward the cabinet for a glass to fill with water I didn't really want. But I needed to act like I was doing something other than trying to get away from her questions. "That's why I went outside."

She stopped and watched me. Maybe she decided to give me a Christmas dispensation. I felt the tension evaporate. "You know," she said, "if we'd put those cameras up, this wouldn't happen."

"Maybe I will," I said, taking another drink of tap water. It felt warm in my mouth. I wanted to spit it out.

"I'm going back to bed," she said, and she began to walk away. "Nice job on the bike," she added as she disappeared onto the staircase.

I thought she was being sarcastic, since I'd gotten none of Macy's big gift for the year assembled before they showed up. I looked down. The collection of parts was gone.

I stepped into the TV room. There it was. Fully assembled. Ready to go. It even had a bow on it. I put my hands on the seat, trying to make sure the thing was real. I'd done a good job. If I'd even done it. If I didn't, who in the hell did?

I sat on the couch, in the same spot where my father had been sitting. I replayed the entire exchange with my parents and the conversation with my brother, multiple times. I wanted to write it all down, but I didn't want Linda to ever find the notes. Maybe I'd tell her I had an idea for a Christmas story that nobody would ever find remotely believable. Then again, millions suspend disbelief every year when taking in the Christmas Eve adventures of George Bailey and Ebenezer Scrooge. Why would anyone regard the past few days in the life of John Persepio as impossible?

But it was impossible. All of it. *I really do have a brain tumor*, I thought. That could be the only explanation for any of it. I was hallucinating.

What about Macy? She had seen them. She knew who they were. Who they weren't. They weren't the Alexanders. Maybe the hallucination included believing someone else was experiencing it, too. Or maybe she had the same brain tumor I had.

It was all so crazy. I kept working my way back through the interactions with three people who had been dead for years. It was clear, and it was consistent. It had happened. It was real. Maybe it was just a really good hallucination. How many more of those would I have?

This time, I felt it coming. I hustled to the bathroom on the other side of the kitchen before vomiting into the toilet, as quietly as I could. (Not very.) After it was over, I stood at the sink. I washed my hands. I caught my reflection in the mirror above the basin. I could see all three of their faces in mine, one after the other. My brother. Then my father. Finally, my mother. I sat down on the wooden floor and started to cry.

"What have I done," I said through tears that wouldn't stop. "What have I done?"

The next thing I saw was daylight, making its way from the window over the sink and through the open door to the bathroom. I figured I'd slept, but it didn't feel like I was waking up. I pushed myself from the floor. My knees wobbled. There was a small stain from a splash of puke on my pants. I threw my left hand against the wall until I was steady. In the mirror, it was just my own face, outlined in white stubble.

"Ho, ho, ho," I said before exiting to the kitchen. I could see snow falling outside. Large flakes that danced in defiance of gravity. Was it really snowing? I had begun to doubt everything I saw. But at least I knew it was Christmas morning.

I resolved then and there to put it all out of my mind. It was the only way to ensure the day would unfold exactly the way it needed to go. I made it my sole focus.

I looked down and saw Buster, peering up at me. There was something in those black eyes, like he knew exactly what had happened, what would happen. I put my hand on top of his head and left it there. His tail wagged softly. I took it as him telling me everything would be all right, because I needed to hear that from someone, anyone.

I was determined the kids would remember this Christmas as a good one. Maybe the last good one they'd have, until they had kids of their own.

That's exactly how it would go. From the time Macy rambled down the stairs and threw her arms around her bike shouting "thank you Sthanta!" over and over again. Linda soon entered, smiling at Macy's glee. The boys made from their bedrooms not long after, no sign of the devices that normally kept them hypnotized, no graceless exit to the basement to fire up their video game. We gathered in the TV room around the tree, basking in the joy that emanated from Macy. I felt nourished by it. I got the feeling the others did, too.

We settled into the routine of unwrapping gifts, with Macy opening hers before Mark and then Joseph. I watched all of it, gathering the torn papers and collecting them in a heap while they enjoyed an occasion that wouldn't last very long but that hopefully would live forever in their memories, especially in mine.

After it all ended, I started for the kitchen to get a garbage bag.

"Daddy," Macy said, "there's one for you."

She brought me a package. It wasn't big. It felt solid and firm.

"Who's this from?" I said. Linda made a face of confusion. It didn't seem very persuasive. Then again, I'd lost my ability to read her, if I ever even had it. The boys, on the other hand, were easy; it was clear they had nothing to do with it.

"It'sth for you. It has your name on it. Sthee? It sthays John."

"It actually says Johnny," I said. "Who calls me Johnny?" Macy giggled as I said my name in a way none of them ever used it, not even Linda.

I unwrapped the present slowly. The covering seemed old and worn, unlike anything from the long tubes Linda had collected over the years. Underneath the wrapping paper was a white box. I held it in my hands.

"Earth to Daddy," Macy said. I looked at her. "Open it, Johnny." She laughed as she said it.

In her laughter, I could hear my brother's laugh. Had I never noticed she laughs just like he did?

I found the bottom of the lid and pulled it away. It was a

picture frame, turned upside down. I lifted it. I started crying all over again.

"What'sth wrong, Daddy?"

I showed her the picture. It was my parents, Baby Michael, and me. Taken by my grandmother on a Christmas, years ago. We were all flashing broad, open-mouthed smiles, as if someone had told a funny joke right before a flash of light had exploded and the shutter had snapped.

Linda walked over to look at the photo. "Do you know who those people are?" she said to Macy.

She focused on the image. It was just a hair out of focus. "That's Daddy in the middle," Macy said. "And those are the old people."

"Which old people?" Linda said.

Macy spirited away, back toward her bike. "The old people we sat with in church. But they were a lot younger then. Like you and Daddy now."

"Thank you," I said to Linda as the wetness made its way down my cheeks.

"Don't thank me," she said. "Seriously, I don't know where that came from. Boys, did you do this?"

They both shrugged at her.

"Macy, where did this come from?" Linda said.

She shrugged, too, not because she didn't know the answer but because she knew it was clear and obvious.

"Sthanta," she said.

And then she hopped on her bike.

31

I ATE AS much food as I wanted to eat. I drank as much wine as I wanted to drink. I lived for the day. For that day. I cleared a spot for the photograph on the mantle, and I found myself staring at it throughout the morning, afternoon, and evening.

I helped with the meal preparations, zealously and diligently and without complaining a single time. Linda had decided to salvage the ham Buster had defiled. I carefully sliced pieces from the bone, so that our guests wouldn't endure the imperfect presentation of a dinner-table centerpiece missing a conspicuous chunk that would soon be deposited somewhere in the backyard.

The house hummed with the full-blown happiness of Christmas. Everything felt different, special. I didn't even brace myself for something to go haywire. I knew in my heart that it wouldn't. Even if that was a hallucination, too, I welcomed it.

Nothing bothered me. Nothing. Linda's parents were a joy. The other guests, including the snot-nosed nephews who knew how to push my buttons and loved doing it, warmed my heart. I wanted the day to be perfect, and perfect it was. Sure, there were a few minor things that on any other occasion would have left me feeling irritated. Not this time. Not this day.

Could it have been even more perfect? Sure. Linda and I could have rekindled the portion of our relationship that had filled the house with children. But I accepted that this ship had sailed, and I knew the direction it was heading. Trying to use the magic of Christmas to alter the inevitable would have only undermined the day. I knew my fate. I accepted it. I welcomed it.

I woke up early Tuesday morning, and I remembered that Earl Matherson had expected me to show up that same day to give them a rehearsal of my closing argument. I called Sandy and asked as nicely as I could if we could postpone it until Wednesday. I heard the line go quiet as she pressed the mute button on her phone so that she could run it by Earl. Whatever she (or he) said next, I wasn't going. But I didn't want him to be upset with her about it. When she returned, she asked me if I could be there at five o'clock the next after-noon. I smiled as I promised that nothing would keep me from being there. Well, almost nothing.

I retrieved the newspaper, flipping through the ever-thin-ning collection of local stories that had no viable home on the Internet. I read the obituaries, studying the pictures of the dear departed and the prose accompanying the official announcements that they had gone wherever they go, learn-ing whatever they learned, doing whatever they do.

It was obvious which ones were written by a family member and which ones had been pounded out by a low-level staffer who had studied journalism in college with slightly greater career aspirations in mind. Would the person who typed up the perfunctory details of the passing of Robert Lee Ashwell, 85, ever achieve what he or she wanted before someone else summarized the surviving family members of him or her? Had I? Had anyone?

How many people get to the end of the road with no regrets, having done everything they ever wanted to do, experienced everything they wanted to experience, seen everything they wanted to see? Most expect they'll have more time than they get. Most wanted, quietly or not, something more or different from what they got. At the end, does it even matter? Rich or poor, tall or short, handsome or ugly, thin or fat, happy or sad, fulfilled or empty, the end comes for us all. A small handful are remembered beyond the boundaries of their own circle of family and friends. Once it's all over, does that matter, either?

I sat there thinking about those things and others until I heard Macy's small legs working their way from upstairs. She smiled at me, and I smiled back. I started crying again.

"Daddy, why are you sthad?"

"I'm not sad, Macy. I'm happy."

"Why are you happy?"

"Well, I'm happy because we're going to make pancakes."

"You mustht really like pancakesth."

I laughed and got up, scooping her from the ground and carrying her to the kitchen. Wrapping my arm around her skinny torso and dipping her down and lifting her up and listening to her cackle every step of the way. She helped me make a big batch of pancakes, enough to feed the family several times over. I dropped a few toward Buster, pretending each time that it was an accident. Macy laughed, sounding more and more like my brother, every time I said "oops" and Buster gobbled up a small, thin circle of grilled dough.

I asked her to go get Linda and the boys, to tell them

we had pancakes and I wanted everyone to have breakfast together. She relished being given a project, and she darted upstairs. Buster ordinarily would have followed her, but there were more pancakes. I fed him another one or two by hand before getting the syrup properly heated in the microwave and setting the table. I clanged the dishes and utensils with a little more gusto than necessary, hoping to reinforce the message Macy would be delivering.

I knew there was a chance Mark and Joseph wouldn't make it down. I decided not to let it bother me if they didn't show up. I didn't want them to think anything was amiss, and the last thing I wanted was for them to ever feel any regret about skipping what I'd hoped would be one final special family occasion before change came abruptly, decisively, and permanently.

The table was set. Wisps of steam rose from the syrup. The pancakes were on a large plate I'd slid into the oven, set on a temperature high enough to keep them warm but low enough to keep them from drying out.

I decided we'd eat at the big table. I lifted the plates and walked into the dining room. I began whistling *Silver Bells*. I got to the table and put the stack down on the surface.

"You making enough for us?"

I looked up, and there they were. All three of them. My father sat at one end, fedora on his lap, overcoat still on. He'd licked his fingers and was working unsuccessfully on smoothing his bristly white hair. To his right was my mother, sitting and smiling at me.

My brother was across from her. He wasn't quite smiling, but he wasn't frowning, either. The lightning bolt was gone from above his eyebrow, and he looked far less like the skinny, wiry figure and more like the man who had last been inside my house the day before he died.

"I love the smell of pancakes," my brother said.

"You always preferred French toast," my mother said.

"I can make some if you want," I said to my brother.

"We won't be staying long enough to eat," she said.

My father frowned at that. "I could really go for some flap-jacks," he said.

"We don't have time," she said. "You know that."

"How did you like the picture?" my father said.

"How do you know about that?"

"Where did you think it came from? Santa Claus?"

I looked at my mother. Her smile was even broader. "I've been carrying that around for a long time. I like where you put it."

"My face looks weird in it," my brother said.

"That's because the two of you were monkeying around," my father added. "But I didn't mind. I knew it was the only way both of you would end up smiling."

"What did we do?" I said.

"You don't remember?" Michael said.

"It's not a quiz," I said. "I truly don't remember."

"You sang that song you were just whistling," my mother said.

"Silver bells, my butt smells," my father sang in a choppy, uneven voice.

It came back to me. I started laughing. My brother did too, sounding more like Macy than himself.

My mother put her hand over her mouth, as she often did when something amused her. It was something that didn't happen often, and I remembered how happy it made me when I'd find a way to make her laugh.

The moment passed, and I saw my father put his hat back on. "Well," he said. "It's time."

"Just like that?"

"We don't make the rules," he said.

He stood first, then my brother. He walked around the table and helped my mother to her feet. The three of them stood there. I watched them. They watched me. I knew they were waiting for me. I walked toward them, and the four of us wrapped our arms around each other in a group hug that hadn't happened in a very, very long time, possibly not since the day the photo on the mantle was taken.

I closed my eyes in their embrace. A rush of memories flooded my mind, quickly and slowly at the same time. Mornings and evenings and outings and dinners and parties and trips in the car and every experience we'd ever shared during the short time, in the grand scheme of things, we'd shared a home.

I lost track of time. It could have been seconds. It could have been hours. It could have been years. I began to understand what Michael had been explaining to me. I felt fully within however they'd been existing since the fundamental change in their existences had occurred.

I dropped my arms and stepped away without intending to do it; it happened when it was supposed to happen. I opened my eyes. They were gone.

I stood there, wondering whether I'd done the right thing. Whether I'd made the right decision.

And then Macy came skipping into the dining room.

"They're coming," she said. "I told them we're having pancakesth, and they sthaid they're coming."

32

I PULLED INTO the driveway. The sky was blue. The air was crisp. Christmas once again was only three days away.

We'd settled into a routine. Instead of knocking on the door or blowing the horn or calling anyone, I'd send a one-word text to Linda. *Here.* That was the code, the signal, the trigger that would result in one or more of the kids emerging from the front door and making their way to the car. The Subaru had been traded for an Audi. I spent more on it than I should have. But it had been a good year.

Financially, that is. The divorce was finalized quickly, and so it had been a good year for Linda, too. That was fine by me. I didn't fight any of it. When I decided to stay, I decided to accept whatever would happen. And it was my fault. I accepted that, too. Everything was my fault. She didn't fall out of love with me; I pushed her there. I had to live with that, and I would never be upset with her for a natural reaction to the way I'd behaved for all those years.

Could I have gotten a better settlement if I'd told my lawyer to go full-blown, razor-toothed barracuda? Probably. I didn't care. I wanted Linda and the kids to have more than enough. They deserved it.

I'd finally decided to start advertising on TV, to start taking on injury cases. Someone needed to do it. Why not me? I'd already settled several of them, and the money was strong. As usual, Linda had been right.

Sandy Matherson's case remained caught in the gears of the appellate process. The verdict would continue to generate more interest than the money would have earned in any low-risk investment, so that was fine by me, too. U-Sav-Plentee threw the Hail Mary pass after losing at trial, because the company always did. Because it could. Barring something completely unexpected, I'd be entitled to forty percent of $2.4 million. But for my divorce—and but for Earl being a gratuitous jerk—I would have cut my fee. Not this time. I had earned every penny. And then some. Plus, I needed whatever I could get for the monthly nut I had to surrender, by decree of the family court judge. Again, I didn't mind any of it.

We technically had joint custody of the kids. But I didn't want to disrupt their routine. I'd swing by whenever, wherever. Sometimes with not much notice. Linda was grateful I didn't push to have them spend the night more often at my new place, so she never resisted any of my requests to pick up one or more of the kids for a few hours. I tried to spend more and more time with them individually, in order to have a strong relationship with each child. I realized by November I'd done more actual parenting over the past year than I had during all of their lives combined. Maybe this really was a good thing.

And I didn't have a brain tumor, after all. The CAT scan and the MRI were clear. Blood tests were fine. The doctors

concluded it was something called Meniere's disease. I'd
never heard of it, one of the many conditions there isn't one
specific test to diagnose, that they just conclude that's what it
is after ruling out everything else it could be. Inner ear situation. It was causing the sudden bouts of nausea. The doctors
were surprised I didn't have vertigo. I didn't tell them about
the hallucinations, if that's what they were. I took some med-
ication for a while and it got better.

The hallucinations had stopped, if that's what they were.
I didn't see my father, my mother, or my brother again. And
nothing else unusual occurred. Time passed, other issues
intervened, and the memory of whatever had happened
those few days in late December of the prior year began to
fade.

Macy hurried down the walkway from the front stoop a
few minutes after I'd sent the text. She was bigger, but not
by much. Her hair was longer and slowly getting darker. It
seemed destined to land on a shade somewhere between
mine and Linda's, just as the boys' had.

Macy climbed into the back of the car, behind the front
passenger seat, so that she could see me more easily when we
talked. She badly wanted to be old enough to sit up front, but
she accepted the rules. "Hi Daddy," she said. "I can't believe
it's going to be Christmas in only three days."

"It always flies by," I said. "Wait until you're old like me."

"You're not old, Daddy."

"I'm old enough."

"Old enough to what?"

"To feel old," I said. "And to know I'm old. But that's fine.
We all get old, if we're lucky."

"What's that mean?"

"Nothing," I said, thinking of Michael and trying not to
wonder what it was that made him choose to go without

getting the same choice I'd had (if any of that was real), regretting that I didn't ask him when I had the chance. Our conversation happened so fast that night (if it happened), and it really wasn't about him. It was about me and my decision. It wasn't real, I reminded myself. So even if I'd asked him about it, whatever he would have said wouldn't have been real, either.

"Earth to Daddy," Macy said, smiling. Her catchphrase from a year ago had morphed into an inside joke we would always share. I turned to face her. She was looking more and more like Linda, but I was starting to see something emerging that was going to make her even prettier, more passionate, more complicated. Maybe someone whose husband would know what he had and not screw it all up.

"So where are we going, Daddy?"

The lisp was gone. Linda finally agreed to prioritize it, maybe because I didn't fight any of the divorce stuff. A couple months of speech therapy, and it was gone. Like it was never there.

"We're going to my hometown. We're going there for the afternoon."

"Is it far?"

"About a hundred miles. Is that OK?"

"Can we listen to Christmas songs on the way?"

I turned up the volume on the radio. *The Little Drummer Boy* happened to be playing.

"Pa-rum-pum-pum-pum!" she squealed, with a little laugh that reminded me of my brother, just like every other time I'd heard her laugh since the first time I'd noticed it last Christmas.

We drove and talked and listened to Christmas songs. She sang the ones she knew, and she pointed out to me the ones she didn't. She asked me questions about growing up, about my parents and my brother. When we weren't talking I was trying to think of the right way, if there was one, to ask her about the old man and his wife. I didn't want to say too much, but I was also curious about what she remembered, if she remembered anything. If she actually saw them at all or whether it really was an extremely elaborate hallucination.

After nearly an hour in the car, I blurted it out. "Macy, do you remember those people we sat with at church last year?"

"The Alexanders?"

"Yes," I lied. "The Alexanders. What do you remember about last year?"

"We saw them at the store, right? When we were buying all the stuff for the tree."

"Yes, we did."

"Weren't they supposed to come to the house for Christmas dinner?"

"You invited them," I said. "I definitely remember that."

"I can't remember why they didn't come," she said.

I stole a glance in the rearview mirror. I could see her scrunching her face together, same as she always did when thinking hard. "They ate with us at Christmas Eve breakfast, too. Right?"

I nodded. I could feel my eyes getting wet, just a little bit.

"They came and sat with us at church," she said. "I sat between them. They were so nice."

"Yes. They were." I turned my head a bit to the left as I drove, hopeful she wouldn't notice I was getting emotional, something I didn't expect and something I didn't want to explain.

"You know how I know you're not old, Daddy?"

"How's that, honey?"

"You remember things. Old people don't remember things."

"Why do you say that?"

"Well," she said, "they're old. When I saw them at church the next time and I said hello to them, I don't think they remembered me."

I sat there for a few miles of the drive, thinking about that one and saying nothing. Thinking about what it potentially meant to whatever it was I'd experienced, starting exactly one year ago that same morning.

"It was weird, Daddy. I went up to them and started talking to them. They looked the same, but they didn't act the same. That's when I knew old people sometimes don't remember things."

I nodded without saying a word.

"So you're not old, Daddy. Because you remember things."

We went back to singing Christmas songs for the rest of the drive, until I took the exit that led to the neighborhood where I'd grown up. We drove by our house. It seemed smaller than I remembered, and some of the others had gotten a little run down. But the neighborhood had that same familiar feel. I caught myself looking around to see if maybe they were wandering the streets, or if that big Chevy was parked somewhere. I was both happy and sad to not see any sign of them.

I drove around town to show her the places I knew so well. The small Catholic school where I'd spent so many of my days. The church next to it. She wanted to see it. I took her inside. It felt, it looked, and it smelled exactly the same as it always did. Two distinct phases of my life intersected, without incident. They coexisted, not collided.

I kept looking for them. I saw nothing. I felt nothing. They were gone.

We're on our way home.

They were home. Whatever had happened last year, they were home.

I checked my phone. We had enough time to get there before sunset. I still thought about skipping the last stop. Once we were in the car and back on the road, I decided to go. For the first time since they buried my brother across from my parents.

I hadn't told Linda I'd been thinking about taking Macy to the cemetery. Maybe Linda expected I would stop there. She knew me well enough to know I wouldn't go back without visiting their graves. But I didn't want to traumatize Macy so close to Christmas. So I decided I'd simply explain to her where we were going, and to give her a chance to say she didn't want to do it.

She didn't object. She seemed curious. And it's not as if kids never go to a place like that, I told myself. She needed to go someday. Today was the right day to do it.

The Audi rolled through the entrance. The front of the cemetery contained the many graves that no one ever visited. The dates on some of the stones were jarring to see. They'd been there a hundred years or longer. I thought back to last year. I wondered where all those people were.

As the car rolled deeper into the field of granite markers or various shapes and sizes, the dates became more recent. I saw a few other cars parked, with one or two people cleaning stones and adorning them with holly or leaving a potted poinsettia. I struggled to remember exactly where they were, but as we got closer, it came back to me. There was one particularly unusual headstone, a large black marker turned into a diagonal that always served as the reminder to me of the right location. I parked the car and popped the trunk.

"You don't have to come with me, if you don't want to."

"I do, Daddy. I want to see where grandma and grandpa are. And Uncle Michael."

Hearing her say those words caused my eyes to well again.

I got out of the car and went to the back. I removed the small box I'd tucked inside and waited for Macy. She didn't ask me what I had.

She recognized it was a place for quiet, for solemnity and respect. It made me proud. It made me think that, years from now, maybe she'd be bringing her own child to visit me in a place like that. Maybe in that exact same place. I'd never really thought about where I'd be buried. I'd considered cremation. In that moment, I decided not to deprive her of the chance to have a specific place where she could see me, whenever she wanted to. Even if she rarely ever did.

She reached for my hand as we moved with slow, soft steps over the ground. The grass was softer than it should have been in late December. It allowed us to move in silence toward the destination.

I noticed that someone had been buried that same day, a few rows over. Two men were dismantling the tent that had been erected for the service. They were carrying the pieces toward a truck that had the name of the cemetery painted in block letters on the side.

I turned back and saw the stone, with my parents' first names next to each other under our last name, in all capitals.

Macy pointed with her free hand and said, "Grandma and grandpa."

We stopped in front of it. I was crying. I noticed Macy was, too.

"It's OK, Macy. They've been gone a long time."

"But why do they have to be in the ground? In the dark? Are they scared?"

"They're not. They're not down there. That's just who they used to be."

Tears rolled over her cheeks, spilling out from behind her glasses. "So where are they?"

"They're home, Macy. They're home."

I turned to the other side of the row, where Michael was buried. I saw the year he was born. I could recall for a vivid instant the moment they walked through the front door with him. I saw the year he died. I pushed away any memories from that part of it.

I pulled the box open. It was the picture I'd gotten last Christmas. I bent over and placed the frame at the base of his stone, propping it up and making sure it stayed firmly in place.

Macy smiled when he saw it. She then looked confused. "Don't you want to keep it?"

"This is a different one. I still have the other one."

"Is he home, too, Daddy?"

"He is," I said to her.

"Was he nice?"

"He was. He would love you so much. You remind me of him."

"Do you think he sees me?"

"I know he does. They all do. Every day."

"I wish I could see them."

"You will. But that will happen a long, long time from now."

She seemed to be happy about that, despite the implication. We stood there for a while, not saying anything. I said a silent prayer. I asked him to forgive me for not coming sooner, for forgetting about him for all those years.

We walked back to the car, hand in hand. We'd both stopped crying.

"Where are we going next, Daddy?"

"We're going home, Macy. And you're going to have a good Christmas."

"Not like last year, when you lived with us."

"Every Christmas is a good Christmas," I said.

I helped her inside the back seat of the car, and I got in

front. The men were still working, carrying the pieces of the tent back to the truck. One of them was skinny, with scraggly hair and a ratty mustache.

The setting sun caught something above his eyebrow. It glistened. I squinted to see what it was.

I smiled at him.

He smiled back at me and waved.

Made in the USA
Coppell, TX
07 November 2023

23910448R10149